THE JADE THRONE

Book 3 in the *Land of Iyah* trilogy

CHRISTA YELICH-KOTH

COPYRIGHT

This book is a work of fiction. All characters and events portrayed in this book are either products of the author's imagination or are used fictitiously.

THE JADE THRONE
Book 3 in the *Land of Iyah* trilogy

SPECIAL THANKS

Mom: For your incredible edits and ability to help me get this done!

Dad: For your speedy beta reading when I really needed it and your great feedback.

Conrad Teves: For helping me create a stunning and beautiful cover.

And to you, the reader: Your interest and love of my books allows me to keep writing more stories. Thank you! I hope you enjoy the conclusion to this trilogy!

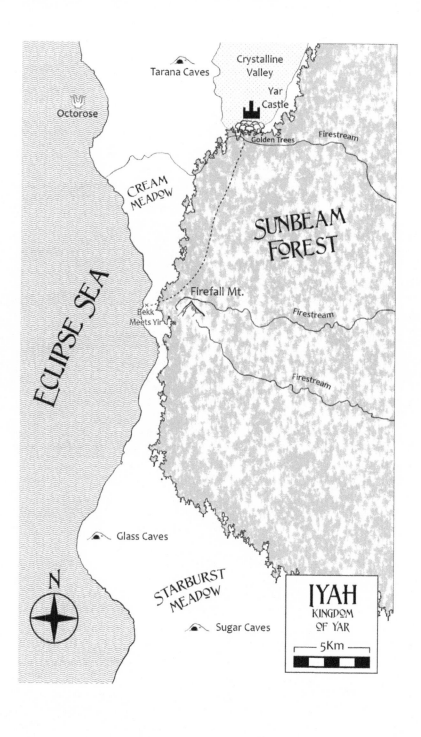

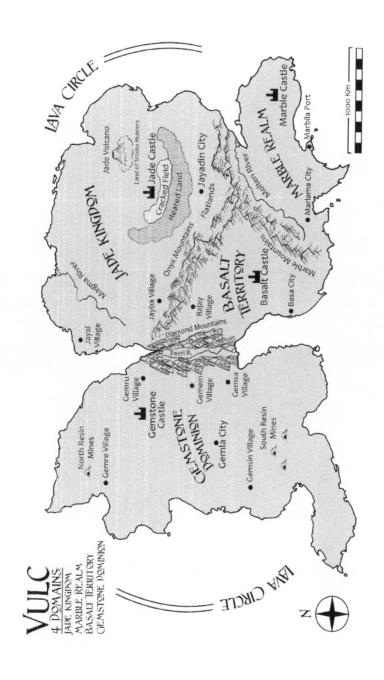

CHAPTER 1

Mania swept over Shon. With quick but soft steps, he paced next to his bed in the psych ward of the Marvin Looshe Medical Facility. Only the hum of the heater nearby and the soft snoring of the other person in the room could be heard.

What did this mean? Why had he heard his brother's voice when he'd been on the brink of sleep?

The young man in the nearby bed groaned and rolled over. Shon halted in his steps, holding his breath, until he heard his roommate's slow and steady breathing resume.

Shon sunk onto the edge of his bed, the once foreign sheets now familiar. He'd been in this facility for nearly five months, arriving after his brother's death at the beginning of the summer.

He remembered the horrible day with crystal clarity. After confronting Bekk in Iyah, his younger brother had given up his life in the real world to keep Shon out of the dream world. When he awoke, Shon discovered the truth of what had happened in that other land: his brother's body lay unmoving and lifeless.

Without any parents and no nearby family, Shon had

panicked. First, he called his girlfriend, Treena. She told him to stay calm, that she would call the police, and he should start CPR on Bekk.

Shon returned to Bekk's room, blindly following Treena's advice, but once there, he knew any resuscitative measures would be futile. Bekk had chosen this path. He couldn't return to his body. He *wouldn't*.

After that, the memories blurred together. Shon recalled Treena arriving, her face tear-streaked and red, and shortly after, the police. They'd removed Bekk's body and took Shon downtown for questioning.

Shon didn't even remember exactly what he'd said. He'd babbled incoherently, talking about Iyah and saving his parents and that Bekk wouldn't understand about how things worked there, what the arch really was, and the dangers of that world.

It didn't take long for the police to recommend hospitalization at Marvin Looshe. They thought finding his younger brother dead had broken him. The State, who'd been watching Shon's living situation closely since his and Bekk's parents had died and Shon had been instated as his brother's guardian, determined he'd become unstable. They issued an order that Shon must attend three months of mandatory in-patient hospitalization at Marvin Looshe, with a standing order that he not be released until deemed functional by a physician.

Shon spent the first few days in the hospital mostly talking to himself. No one believed the truth.

And why should they? Why would anyone believe his brother

had died to stop Shon from killing fairies in a dream world?

During the first few weeks, Shon had resisted everything in the hospital. He hated the place. He'd been Bekk's guardian for nearly two years since their parents' death. Because of this, he'd become fiercely independent. He'd learned how to handle a budget, how to earn a living for them both, keep Bekk on task with chores and homework, have a girlfriend, and manage a household. The restrictions imposed on him—when to sleep and wake up, when and what to eat, a structured day filled with therapy and programmed events—grated against him. But in a place like this, resistance was met with medication modification. Sedatives were a doctor's best friend for dealing with unruly patients.

The weeks stretched into a month. The pills kept him quieter. He didn't mind that. He went through his day, kept to himself. He never volunteered information during the therapy sessions. Social interactions were minimal at best.

Visitors then became allowed. Treena showed up. At first, Shon had been thrilled, not only that she still loved him, but because he had some contact with the outside world. Their meetings, though brief, filled him with joy.

Her visits, however, also brought on a new feeling he hadn't expected: guilt. She reminded him of the life he used to have, and how he'd ruined it all.

Including leading his own brother to his death.

Every time she left, the pain of not having access to anyone outside these walls ate at him. By the time another month rolled through and summer came to an end, he could feel the strain emanating from her as well. Her visits seemed more like someone who felt obligated, like she'd feel guilty if she *didn't* come to see him. Their talks became haphazard at best. He didn't have new news, and she stopped telling him about her life.

Because she was moving forward. Something he couldn't do.

Before Bekk's passing, she had planned to live with the brothers. Now? She'd left home and moved into a dorm room at the college she attended. She'd made new friends. Shon had a feeling she only came to see him now out of a sense of responsibility.

The only other visitor had been his grandmother, on his mother's side. She hadn't seen him often, merely twice in the past two months, but she'd seemed genuinely concerned for Shon's wellbeing. Tension sat between the two of them, due to the fact his grandmother had cut ties with the family a long time ago. Besides that, though, seeing her reminded Shon that his mother was no longer around, and shame once again infiltrated his thoughts.

At that point, depression and anxiety took over. The panic of being trapped in this facility for the rest of his life plagued him and yet the fear of returning to the real world overwhelmed him. A sense of where he belonged eluded him. He sought out the prescribed drugs. Anything to make him not miss his old life.

He let the medication nibble away at his soul, allowing the hollowness to consume him from the inside out.

Then a few weeks ago, three teenagers accompanied Treena on her weekend visit. They'd been Bekk's friends. He hadn't even paid attention to them at first until one of them, Ashlee, told him they knew about Iyah and that she'd been instructed to help Bekk.

Adrenaline spiked through the medicated haze. They knew about Iyah? How?

After that conversation, Shon spent the entire week not taking his medication in order to keep a clear head, eagerly awaiting a chance to talk to the three of them the following weekend. He couldn't believe someone else knew about Iyah. And, perhaps, there could be a way to save his brother.

During their next visit they'd asked Shon questions, which he diligently answered, but his time limit with visitors at the hospital made it difficult to fill them in on all he wanted them to know. After this second visit, in which they updated him about Bekk and the stone world's king who was trying to reopen the arch inside Iyah, Shon crafted a letter, detailing everything he knew or could remember about the dream land, so he could give them the pages at their next meeting. He'd found a loose tile in the bathroom and had hidden the papers there. The last thing he wanted was for anyone to find out he not only still believed in Iyah, but that he was comprising notes about the place.

Now, it was the following weekend. Bekk's three friends planned to try that very night to fall asleep and visit the world of Iyah. Then, tomorrow, they would return to the hospital for the third time and tell Shon about it. At that point, he'd give them the letter.

Shon had laid in bed that night, thinking about his brother, hoping the information he'd given so far to Bekk's friends would be of some help. He'd drifted in and out of sleep, until words sounded in his mind, as if on the wrong end of a funnel. They sounded tinny and scratchy, but he couldn't mistake the voice.

It was Bekk.

He said, *"Okay, let's see what we know."*

Shon had bolted awake, searching the room frantically, but only dimness and the smell of a sterile room hit his senses.

Now, too awake to fall back asleep, Shon paced. He knew he wasn't allowed to enter Iyah again while Bekk existed there, but if he could hear his brother...

Had something changed?

And if so, could Shon use this to his advantage to *send* a message?

Could he help undo the damage he'd done and bring Bekk home?

CHAPTER 2

Bekk felt like a coward. A lonely, frustrated, shameful coward.

Two days ago, he'd been ruler of the land of Iyah, king of Yar Castle. Now, he sat on a beach, alone, too scared to return to the palace because a huge man made out of jade stone had come from another world with dozens of soldiers and seized the place and its throne.

Bekk knew he shouldn't feel shame or cowardice. He was only a seventeen-year-old guy, after all. What could he do against an army made of rock?

And yet, guilt chewed at his insides. A month ago he'd given up his life on Earth to stop his brother's reign here and take over the throne. Except now, he didn't have another life to relinquish in order to banish this stone king from Iyah, too. And even if he did, he couldn't get rid of all the soldiers on his own.

Instead, he'd run. Calling all the fairies who lived inside the castle, he'd dashed away from the terrifying black arch that sprouted in his bedroom, which produced jade body after jade body as the soldiers marched through the void from their own world into

Iyah.

The only thing that made him feel a little better had been the addition of his two friends, Belle and Vic. They'd arrived just as Bekk had fled the castle and made the journey with him west to the Eclipse Sea.

When they came to the beach, Belle and Vic assured him they'd help to reclaim the palace, saying that maybe the information they'd learned about the stone world from his brother, Shon, would help.

Unfortunately, right at that moment, the two of them disappeared from Bekk's side, which meant they'd woken up in their own world.

Time worked differently in Iyah than on Earth, so Bekk had no idea how long it would be until his friends returned. *If* they returned. There were no guarantees they even could. After all, his girlfriend, Ashlee...well, he *hoped* she thought of herself as his girlfriend...hadn't come with Belle and Vic this last time, even though they'd all planned to return together.

Bekk thought of Ashlee and let out a big sigh. He hoped she was okay. Worry crept through him. What if he never saw her again? What if, for some reason, she couldn't return to Iyah? A sinking feeling of ominous despair trickled through him. Something inside felt almost certain he'd never see her in this place again...

With a shake of his head, Bekk got rid of that dark thought. It wouldn't help him in his current situation. Except...what *could* help him?

The fairies he'd amassed outside the castle—around two

hundred or so—had all abandoned him on the beach. They weren't restricted by legs to carry them around. Besides, they had charges to attend to: children who entered into Iyah through their dreams and needed their help.

His closest fairy friend, Ryf, had left as well. The last time Ashlee showed up here (*don't think about it!*) she'd told Ryf she'd seen the fairy's best friend, Yir. Ryf had been very worried about Yir. When Bekk used his own life energy to send away his brother, all the fairies Shon had killed returned to life—except Yir. Having learned that the little green fairy had spoken to Ashlee renewed Ryf's determination to find her. As soon as she'd deemed everyone was a safe distance from the castle, Ryf had flittered away to search for Yir's location.

So, Bekk once again sat by himself, having no plan, letting the stone man and his soldiers do...whatever they intended to do in the castle. Bekk had a feeling their strategy needed use of the amber throne, which he'd learned had the power to open doors to other worlds. For all Bekk knew, the Jade man had already broken into dozens of worlds, murdered or plundered whatever and wherever he wanted, and there was nothing Bekk could do about it.

Some leader *he'd* turned out to be...

CHAPTER 3

The Jade King was trapped.

A growl of frustration from his lips reverberated throughout the inside of the throne room of Yar Castle.

His guards, in their submissive state, didn't even flinch.

How could he have forgotten the key ingredient? He'd been so excited to have broken through the arch's void and claim the throne of Iyah that he'd completely overlooked the fact he would need the life energy of a fairy to break through to another world.

Not to mention the toll the process took on himself.

And, in correlation to that, the amount of resin he'd need to heal himself.

Of which he had none.

Now he had the cracks along his body to prove it. They ached and stung and he could do nothing to help repair them.

How could he have been so foolish to *not* have brought a supply of resin with him? *Arrogance*, he thought to himself. He'd been more focused on the task and not the consequences. Something he'd struggled with his whole life.

The Jade King had finally fulfilled the prophecy told to him by a Basalt oracle 3,000 years ago...and he had no one to share it with. His Love had crumbled a century ago, his son was dead by his own hand, and his daughter had run away, afraid of her own father. No one remained except the three hundred guards he'd brought with him from his homeland.

Not brought...*forced.* He currently controlled them. They stood before him, mindless automatons, doing nothing but waiting for his orders. The pearly substance his son retrieved from Pearl River currently subsided in his own body, triggered by grief at the loss of his son and the fleeing of his daughter. This grief, if held, could spread to another being and possess them, make them bend to his will. It was how he held control over the soldiers.

Holding onto his grief hadn't been that hard. Even in his moment of victory, despair sloshed throughout his being, since he felt completely and utterly alone.

The Jade King tried to focus on the task at hand. He'd done what he'd been destined to do. Crossed the void. Entered Iyah. Taken control of the throne—which shone amber when he first arrived and now glowed with the greenness of jade stone—and its power to open doors to a plethora of other worlds. Worlds which he planned to invade, to obtain their resources in order to save his own land in the Jade Kingdom.

But the energy needed to do all this had cracked his stone body, leaving grooves along his arms, legs, and chest. His strength, now depleted, left him sitting on the throne feeling old and decrepit.

His guards did nothing to help. There was nothing they *could* do. Their intentions meant nothing because they had none.

The Jade King decided to rest before attempting to enter a new world. Ordering his soldiers to watch for intruders, he tried to sleep, to rejuvenate his body.

But sleep never came. He rested, yes, but he could not succumb to slumber.

"What is this place?" he'd said out loud. "Why can I not sleep here?"

His guards did not answer.

Still, after a day of rest, he did feel better. The cracks had not healed, but they were no longer raw to the touch.

On the second morning, he decided he had enough strength to send a guard home to retrieve some resin for his wounds. However, the soldier returned shortly. The archway, which originally materialized inside one of the bedroom quarters of the castle, had disappeared.

Impossible, he thought. He'd mustered up enough strength to stagger to the room in which the arch had last been, but instead of its vast black space, a solid barrier greeted him. He ran his hands across the wall, but to no avail.

His only way home no longer existed.

Fear crept along his stone skin like beads of trickling lava. He worked his way once again down the hall to the throne room.

If I can't go home through the archway, I will find the door to my world instead. Concentrating, he placed a hand on the throne and felt the power flow through him, picturing his world and the resin deposits he would need.

A door appeared in the throne room, as if it had always been there, just hidden from sight. The Jade King could view through it, noting the volcanic activity before him. He couldn't see anything living, but noted rocks piles of resin deposits just inside the doorway. A longing ached in his chest at the sight of his world. He shook the feeling away and concentrated on the task at hand.

"Grab those," he'd ordered one of the guards. She'd complied by heading towards the doorway. And then...nothing. Her hand stopped at the edge of the entranceway, but she could not reach through the door.

Snarling, the Jade King pushed her out of the way and tried himself. But to no avail. He couldn't reach through either. The barrier felt solid, like a rock wall.

Idiot! he screamed at himself. He couldn't break through the doorway without the life force of a fairy—and they'd all fled from the castle.

The Jade King stumbled into the throne. His breath came in ragged gulps, whether out of exhaustion or fear, he did not know.

He was trapped here, in this world, with no way to return home, no way to heal, and no one else to help him determine what to do next.

The Jade King, a powerful ruler, a man who'd stopped the Gemstone Dominion War by sacrificing his own family, had no idea what to do.

I need someone to talk to.

With delicate concentration, the Jade King focused on the soldier closest to him, Guard Jayrara. He gently released his hold on her, watching the pearly sheen covering her eyes fade away to a look of awareness.

She blinked several times.

"Sire?" she asked, making a slow circle to take in the situation. Huge walls surrounded her, with tendrils of jade seeping through them. The green stone slowly converted the castle's walls, which gave the Jade King more and more power. Chandeliers hung from the ceiling, unlit, and windowed panes allowed light from a green sun to shine through them. "Where am I?"

"Guard Jayrara, you and your fellow guards have crossed through a void with me into another world. We have done so to save our people."

Guard Jayrara's eyes widened. "Another world? Do you mean...are we in the Gemstone Dominion?"

The Jade King shook his head. "No. We are in an alternate world, not of our own. It will supply us with resources to help our people, restore them to what they once were before the war with the Gemstone people."

The Jade King watched her face pinch with confusion and panic.

"I am asleep," she muttered. "Another world? This is not possible." Fear flashed across her face. Her breathing increased rapidly. "No, no this cannot be. I will wake up." She placed a hand on her chest, as if it were constricted.

The Jade King sighed. He hadn't counted on this. He himself had never believed in anything like another world before the Basalt oracle had shown him her vision 3,000 years ago. He'd had all that time to know other worlds existed. But this guard? How could she process this information?

"I apologize," he told her. "I was foolish to think anyone but myself and my family would understand." He concentrated and watched her eyes glaze over again with that same pearly glow. She resumed her normal stance, once again mindlessly under his control.

The Jade King returned to his position on the throne, which fit his large broad body quite comfortably, as if made for him. He needed to think, to plan.

If only he had his daughter, Jayla, here. She'd become quite adept at strategy and planning. After her mother crumbled, she'd taken over the responsibilities of dealing with delegates from other reachable lands, the Marble Realm and the Basalt Territory. Her proposals for treaties had proven quite useful in resupplying their resin stores and her strategies for how to gather information showed she really had a flair on how to maneuver in the realm of politics.

But she was gone. She'd left after telling him she was an oracle.

An oracle. In his own family! And almost within his grasp. The plans he could have concocted, the definitive knowledge if his ideas would work before he did them. A wasted opportunity.

He wondered briefly where she'd gone. Before he'd crossed the void into Iyah he'd sent guards to find her and released WANTED posters for information about her whereabouts.

Unfortunately, since he'd assumed he could return to his own world whenever he pleased, the Jade King hadn't thought about waiting to hear if she'd been located before crossing through the arch into Iyah. Now, he had no idea if she'd been found, if she'd been brought to the castle and waited there under detainment, or if she were even alive.

That is not currently within my power to control, he thought. *I need to focus on what I can do now that I'm here. I must find a way to return home. To do so, I need the life energy of a fairy.*

The Jade King called forth 100 of the 300 guards he'd brought with him.

"I want you to scour the land. Always stay in groups of ten, but fan out around the castle. Do not return until you've captured a fairy. *Alive.*"

The soldiers turned and marched away.

In the meantime, the Jade King focused on what he *could* do. If a fairy couldn't be found, he knew he could still move through the archway and into his world. So, for now, he could bring forth the archway. Except when it had appeared in his own quarters in the Jade Kingdom, it had been because the Basalt oracle had brought it forth. From this end, he didn't know how to do that...

CHAPTER 4

Jayla's gut hurt. The light from the nearest house in front of her—her current destination— danced before her eyes.

"Uhhhh..." she muttered, leaning over in pain.

Basala, the Basalt man Jayla had been following, stopped. He stood about fifty paces ahead.

"What's wrong?" he asked, a tone of annoyance in his voice.

"I'm not sure," she replied, pressing a hand into her abdomen. Another strange pang of twisting pain rotated inside her. "It's my stomach."

"You're probably just 'ungry," he said. "We're almost to shelter. Just 'ang in there." He took off again towards the small lamp in the distance.

Jayla did her best to straighten up, but a fresh lance of pain struck her. It definitely didn't *feel* like hunger. It felt more like...she couldn't quite explain it. All she knew was it was sharp and...and it didn't belong. She followed the best she could, loping behind the Basalt man over the rocky terrain towards an upcoming house.

Basalt rock, being much more porous, broke differently than

jade stone. Instead of smooth breaks and slick sides, the structure they approached appeared more like a carved-out cavern. The basic shape looked rounded, but nothing about it seemed polished. Jayla got the impression it had once been a giant block of basalt which had merely been dug into.

Basala reached the threshold first and rapped smartly on the door. The noise sounded more muffled than Jayla expected, though she took an educated guess that the composition of the basalt rock absorbed sound better. Moments later, the door opened and Basala strode inside, not even waiting for Jayla.

Jayla let out a frustrated grunt. If he was the first person a fleeing refugee met, it would leave the refugee feeling very unwanted and unwelcome.

She ambled the rest of the way, a sheen of sweat across her brow. The light shining through the door looked extremely inviting—a sort of rosy glow that felt different from the reddish-orange glow of lava lamps she normally saw.

Suddenly a figure filled the doorway.

"Why'd you go and leave the poor girl on 'er own, Basala! I swear, you ain't good for nothing much more anymore." The Basalt woman's voice rolled off her tongue, almost as if the words smeared together. Jayla had met a few delegates from the Basalt Territory before and noted their broken words and less formal accents, but this woman's words were the most fractured she'd ever heard.

The woman hustled out of the house and met up with Jayla.

"I'm so sorry, my dear, we'll get you sorted right off now. Don't you worry nothing about Basala. 'E's grumpy. We 'ad three crossers in the past week. Searchers 'ave been upping their game as well. It's got 'im on edge."

Jayla did her best to follow the conversation. She recognized the term "Searchers" from the Basalt man who had helped her cross under the Onyx Mountains the day before. She could only assume they were people who "searched" for members who wanted to flee the Jade Kingdom.

"I don't mean to be a burden," Jayla said, her polite manners kicking in automatically.

"Oh, nonsense. It's nothing about you, dear. You're doing what you gotta to get over 'ere. 'E just needs to retire, but don't know nothing about what else 'e'd do, so 'e's stuck."

They approached the open doorway.

The Basalt woman eyed her. "Are you alright, dear? You seem bent over some."

"My stomach hurts."

"Your..." The woman paused outside the door. "Basala didn't say nothing to that effect."

"The feeling only started since we've walked from the Onyx Mountains. He thought I may be hungry."

The woman narrowed her eyes. "Is it sharp pain? Like shards of broken quartz rolling around in your belly?"

Jayla nodded.

The woman pursed her lips. "Did you 'ave an encounter with a grim-shu in the Onyx mountain pass?"

A sense of surprise crossed over Jayla. "Yes, but it only ripped my bag off my shoulders."

"Mm-hmm." The woman ushered Jayla inside and called across the room in a loud booming voice. "Basala, you idiot! She's been punctured by a grim-shu!"

Jayla wasn't *exactly* sure what that meant, but she knew it couldn't be good.

"'Ow was I to know!" Basala shot at her from the other room. "She said she saw one and it grabbed 'er pack!"

"Fool of a man!" the woman said, shaking her head. "'Ow many 'ours were you waiting for Basala to come?"

"I'm not sure. It was midday when I exited the mountain. When Basala arrived, the moon was out."

The Basalt woman muttered under her breath while she checked Jayla's shoulders. Jayla nervously shifted her torn traveling cape to make sure her Royal mark stayed hidden.

"Yup," the Basalt woman said. "Right 'ere. Base of the neck."

"What is it?" Jayla asked.

"Puncture mark from a grim-shu bite. Its tiny, which may be why you 'adn't felt it right away, not to mention you've got a bunch o' scratches and bruises, probably from your escape."

Jayla could hear the woman's jaw grinding. Then she gave Jayla a pitying look. "Well, there's no two ways about it. You're gonna turn into a grim-shu."

CHAPTER 5

Ashlee stood in shock. Whether more from the statement she'd just heard or from the elaborate room she'd just entered, she wasn't sure. Having resigned to stay in the gem-encrusted castle with a strange Gemstone woman instead of taking her chances alone in an unknown world *seemed* like a good idea at the time, except she didn't feel any less out of place. Besides, she'd seen fantasy movies before, with great halls and elegant ballrooms, but this dining hall? It blew her mind.

A sparkling undulating mosaic composed of red and orange, like an ocean made of lava, flowed across the walls. When Ashlee peered closer, she noticed the makeup consisted of rubies and maybe a type of garnet? The mosaic trailed away into a blur of pinks and reds—rose quartz and more rubies—and ended in a huge figure which appeared to be a volcano made up of onyx and pewter, spewing amethyst. One section seemed out of place though. On the center part of the volcano appeared a large greenish area—a flat stone that didn't quite match all the other sparkling gemstones around it.

Yir, a green fairy from the land of Iyah, who was trapped here as well, peeked out from behind Ashlee's blonde hair.

Everything is very shiny, Yir said, the words appearing like thoughts inside Ashlee's head. *We have sparkly things in Iyah, but nothing this sparkly.* Yir flew off Ashlee's shoulder and settled on the table, admiring her reflection in one of the polished gems of the tabletop.

Once Ashlee finally closed her dropped jaw, she registered the words that had just come from the Gemstone lady in front of her. The Jade King had killed this woman's family.

Ashlee trotted forward, realizing the woman had offered her a chair at the table. "I'm sorry," she muttered. "About what happened to your family." A slight pain shot through her body as she sat on the uneven chair surface. The gemstones, though gorgeous, were not filed or flattened so they kept their contours, some of which were rough to the touch.

The look of malice on the Gemstone woman's face faded away. "It was long ago," she said, her tones dulcet and ethereal. "I was only a gemling at the time. I do not have many memories of them."

Ashlee's eyebrows furrowed. "A gemling? What's that?"

The gemstone lady smiled. "Newly created."

"Oh. Like a baby." Ashlee grinned in understanding. "New to the world."

"Yes." The Gemstone woman swept around to the other side of the table across from Ashlee. Ashlee noted that the woman did not sit at the head. In fact, the two of them sat about three chairs down from the head of the table. Five place settings remained there, polished, but appearing as though they hadn't been moved in centuries.

They probably haven't, Ashlee thought. The sight made her sad. This woman had lived here for three millennia without any family. And yet, she'd been so young. How had she survived?

Before she could ask anything, the Gemstone woman spoke first. "Forgive my bluntness," she said, "but I have many questions about you. For example, I do not know what you are. As well as the creature currently inspecting my family's heirlooms." She said the words with a slight smile, gesturing to Yir who currently flitted amongst the hanging chandeliers.

Ashlee wasn't sure where to begin. She, herself, was new to the notion of other worlds, other beings. Did this woman know about such concepts? Would she understand if explained? Flashes from Ashlee's history class last year sprung to mind: the Inquisition, the Crusades, the Salem Witch trials. People condemned to suffering and death because they spouted different ideas than what were currently acceptable or based on fear of the unknown. Would Ashlee find herself in one of these situations if she said the wrong thing?

And yet, this woman knew about alternate creatures. She'd tamed the black beings inside the arch. She must understand that something lay outside her own world. But how much?

Deciding to play it safe, Ashlee spoke cautiously. "As I said before, my name is Ashlee. I'm called a human. This," she said, pointing to her friend, "is Yir. She's what's known as a fairy."

"You are from the dark land, the land of the archway?"

"No. We are from...somewhere else. I think..." Ashlee paused, trying to make sure she described things correctly. "I think the arch is a gateway to other places. We got caught inside it. That's how your...pets...brought us here."

"Ah, so you are from the land the Jade King seeks to control?"

A sigh of relief escaped her. "So you know about that place? About Iyah?"

"I do. It is where my pets have watched for signs of the prophecy."

"Well I'm not from Iyah, but Yir is. We—"

Suddenly, a small green creature appeared from the greenish section of the wall inside the volcanic mosaic.

Ashlee let out a shriek. "I thought you said you were alone in this castle?" she cried out.

The Gemstone woman gave a weak smile, but her eyes glistened. "I am alone here, as the only Royal to remain, but I do not take care of this castle and its grounds by myself." She nodded to the creature. "This is a Jadari. It lives inside the castle walls. Well, the areas adapted for its existence."

Ashlee reexamined the creature. It had wide eyes and stood about four feet tall with smooth, greenish turquoise skin. "I'm sorry, Jadari," she said. "I've just never seen anything quite like you before."

The Jadari rocked back and forth.

"They do not speak," the Gemstone woman said. "And its name isn't Jadari, that is what its species is called. They do not have individual names. Though it thanks you for your kind words."

"Then how do you address...um...it?"

The Gemstone woman cocked her head slightly, as if thinking. "Surprisingly enough, I have never thought of it. The Jadari simply appear when needed. They are very...protective. They have watched over me since I lost my family. They raised me. While I remained too young to rule, they kept up the appearance of ongoings in the castle. They even sent out a proclamation that the newest gemling, me, was ill, and would need time alone to survive my ailment. It only took ten years for me to become aware enough to be able to help direct the courses of actions for my people."

History class once again floated through Ashlee's brain. She recalled some kingdoms had children as their sovereigns, but they always had advisors to help. This woman had these Jadari to help her, but no one of her own species? What a lonely life.

And yet why? Why didn't they want anyone else to help the Gemstone woman run the kingdom?

Ashlee could think of only one valid reason. They didn't want anyone to know that the Royal Family had died.

"Not to sound offensive," Ashlee began slowly, "but the Jadari look nothing like you. Are they...from somewhere else?"

The Jadari placed a plateful of what Ashlee could only assume was food in front of the woman. The substance looked mostly like ground up stones.

"They usually live in the Jade Kingdom, across the Diamond Mountains. Their bodies are made of jade, so they need access to that stone to stay alive. The Gemstone Dominion does not have natural jade deposits so some were transported here during the early years of my life when the Jadari moved in."

Ashlee noted the green section in the wall, the part that appeared out of place to her. "Is that jade over there?"

"Yes." The woman scooped a section of food from her plate and began...chewing? Ashlee wasn't certain. It looked more like she was grinding her jaw against the food.

Ashlee's forehead wrinkled in confusion about the Jadari. "They didn't live here before?"

"No. They arrived the day after my family died. My memories from then are not very strong, but I remember their comforting presence. The Jadari knew the catastrophe of the Diamond Mountains would happen. That is why they left the Jade Kingdom the year before, crossed the Pearl River, and made a small home for themselves at the northernmost point of the river. They brought stockpiles of jade and created a place in which they could live. Then, when the Diamond Mountains emerged, cutting off their path to the Jade Kingdom, they transported as much jade as they could carry to my castle. They created a space inside the castle walls through which to travel back and forth. But for the most part, they live in a structure to the east of the castle, near the village of Gemru."

Ashlee's head swam from all the information. "I'm sorry. This is a lot for me to figure out."

"Yes. When I first encountered the archway, I was terrified. When I learned there were creatures living inside it, creatures that I could somehow understand, my whole outlook on my world changed. I knew at that moment the prophecy must have been true."

Ashlee, not feeling very hungry, pushed around the rocks on her plate. "That's the second time you've mentioned a prophecy. What was it?"

"My father was the Keeper of Events." She gave a dismissive wave of her hand. "It's a fancy title, but it basically means he kept track of daily activities. There were records of everything that had been decided and implemented by my family. It's how I learned about my family at all, how I knew the Jadari were here to help me.

"As a gemling," she continued, "I was merely a few hundred years old when my family died. When I was of an age to understand, I read through all the recorded events. There had been a war, a great war, that raged for one thousand years before I'd been born. A war my family started."

At this moment, the woman hung her head.

"They started a war?" Ashlee asked tentatively.

"Yes. They believed they had no other choice. An oracle came four thousand years ago and spoke to my family. She told them of a vision she'd had, where the second son of the Jade King would reign over a world of infinite resources and march into the Gemstone Dominion to claim it as his own. My family didn't believe her—prophecies are tricky at best—until a year later when the Jade family announced the birth of a second son. The oracle could not have known about the birth, as creation is a closed ceremony that takes place in mere weeks. For her to have known about it a year in advance?" The woman shook her head. "My family understood at that point the prophecy would come to pass."

"Wow. We have people who...well I guess *they* think they can see the future, but I've never put much stock into it. It's amazing that you have people here who actually *can* see what's going to happen. It must be an incredible ability."

"Perhaps. I would not want it."

Ashlee thought about all the times she would have loved that ability, all the events she could have prevented or prepared for if she knew about them in advance. "Why not? You could see how things are going to turn out."

"In theory, yes. But it is not a way to *always* see the future. The visions are bestowed upon them and they only see what they are shown. They cannot tell what the consequences may be beyond the prophecy, only what they are shown in that moment."

"But your family believed the prophecy?"

The Gemstone woman stirred the rest of the meal around on the plate. "Yes. They set off to discuss what they'd learned with the Jade Family. The talks...did not go well. The Jade people do not believe in oracles. Most oracles come from the Basalt lands, whose people were highly secretive at the time. No one knew much about them. But the Jade Family had already decided the prophecy meant nothing. When my family returned home, the oracle returned in a frenzy. She used her gift to show my mother the prophecy, an act that caused the oracle great personal damage. When my mother saw it, she and the rest of the family decided to...move the Jade child."

A gasp slipped from Ashlee's mouth. "They were going to steal him? How could they do that?"

The Gemstone woman slowly shook her head. "I was also

stunned when I read the Events. How could my family have thought that could possibly be the best action? They, apparently, planned to keep him out of the castle until his one thousandth year. The prophecy showed him accepting his fate inside the Jade Castle. They believed if he wasn't there, it wouldn't come to pass. They had no desire to keep the family away from the child, but they could not let him live inside his own castle. They wanted them to relocate, just for a thousand years. To save everyone. The prophecy my mother saw showed the Jade people in hardship as well. My family wasn't being selfish. They were trying to help the entire land."

"Wow," Ashlee said again, leaning against the chair. "Did they succeed?"

"No. The Jade Family feared us. Protection tripled after our first visit. When our messengers went to give our proposal to the Jade Family, they were imprisoned before they could even be heard. My family assumed the communication had been sent and the Jade Family refused the offer. They didn't know the Jade Family never even heard the proposal. The guards reported that the Gemstone people had tried to murder the Jade Family and war broke out."

"How did you know that the Jade Family never got your message?"

"The Jadari told my family. They live all over the Jade Kingdom, including near the Basalt border. They heard rumors and followed up, learning the truth. They then passed this information on to each other and it spread to the Jade Castle. The Jadari who lived there knew the truth and told the others."

"Then why did the war still happen? Didn't the Jadari tell

everyone?"

"In the Jade Kingdom, the Jadari are servants at the castle, nothing more. They also don't speak. They connect to each other through thought. But even if they *could* tell someone, no one would listen. They would be told to remain silent. If a Jadari goes against whoever they've vowed allegiance to, their bodies melt away and they perish."

Ashlee found the story fascinating. Terrible, but fascinating. She hoped she wouldn't wake up until she got to hear the end of it. But she also realized she could be running out of time and didn't want to leave Yir here, alone, until she knew for sure the little fairy could return home safely to Iyah.

Before she could steer the conversation to a topic that could help Yir, a Jadari burst out of the wall.

"What is it?" the Gemstone woman asked.

The Jadari swayed, then lifted its arms.

"A grim-shu attack? Where?" Tension coated her words.

He made more arm movements.

"Southeast again. In Gemen Village? Very well. We know what to do." The Jadari wiggled then melted into the wall.

Concern spiked through Ashlee. "There's an attack?"

The Gemstone woman nodded, pushing away from the table and standing. "A grim-shu. They are mountain creatures, intangible unless they want to be otherwise. They plague our eastern and southeastern borders."

Ashlee stood as well, following quickly as the Gemstone woman loped from the room.

"Wait! Where are you going?"

"I have to help my people. They will be turned otherwise."

Ashlee slid to a stop. "Turned?"

"Into grim-shu. We must hurry." She fled down the hallway.

Ashlee leaned over to catch her breath. The Gemstone woman, standing at around seven feet tall, moved much faster. She'd already left through the front doors by the time Ashlee reached the edge of the main entranceway.

Yir fluttered up behind Ashlee, landing on her shoulder. *She seems very worried, but very determined.*

Ashlee let out a wheezy laugh. "You are very observant, Yir."

I have always been told that. I can see things other fairies don't put together. I always get the most difficult children. I am the best with them. She paused. *I miss the children. I miss Ryf.*

"I know you do. I'll get you home, somehow." Concern flitted through Ashlee at her statement. What if she woke up before she could return Yir to Iyah? Would her friend be stuck here in this strange world by herself? *I won't leave her,* Ashlee thought. *I have to get her back home before I wake up.*

Secure in the notion that she wouldn't leave her fairy friend behind, she glanced up when two Jadari popped out of a nearby wall. They gestured for her to continue moving forward.

"I suppose they won't let me stay in the castle unattended," Ashlee whispered to Yir.

I can understand that.

"Besides, I'm excited to see more of this world. Might as well until we can figure out how to get out of here."

CHAPTER 6

Bekk heard them before he saw them. The clomping of rhythmic footsteps in the distance. A chill of terror iced its way up his spine.

"No," he muttered. Bekk stood, his feet sinking into the pure white sand. Lavender waves popped behind him across the Eclipse Sea, but they couldn't cover the relentless sound.

The jade soldiers were coming.

Panic flared up inside his chest. Bekk hadn't come up with a plan. There'd been no sign of Ashlee or Belle or Vic. And the fairies had all scattered.

What was he supposed to do?

Crouching down, Bekk hid behind a fallen gold doh-iyah tree next to him. He peeked over it, peering into the distance, the sea's waves lapping at the shore.

Stomp, stomp, stomp, stomp.

There. The soldiers crested into view. He counted about a dozen. They moved in a line, but were slightly apart from each other, as if fanning out in a circle. Soon, they'd reach the beach, and

Bekk would be found.

Bekk's thoughts raced through his mind. Even though he'd existed in Iyah for a little over a month, he'd never explored very far away from the castle. He wracked his brain, focusing on the terrain he knew. To the northeast of him lay the Tarana Caves. They would provide plenty of cover, but he'd have to run towards the soldiers first to clear the coastline. He couldn't move east at all, since that was the direction of the oncoming threat. Behind him, straight west, lay the Eclipse Sea, and he had no clue if there were any land op-tions among its vast, chilly wetness. His only option was to move south along the coastline, which ran adjacent to the Cream Meadow and the Sunbeam Forest. Due south, the forest met the beach and could provide ample cover.

Bekk snuck another glance at the figures marching towards the shore. They appeared methodical, moving at the same pace, and not a quick one. But that didn't mean they wouldn't start running to-wards him if he made a move. Still, if he kept low, he may be able to sprint and get out of their line of sight. Once out of range, he could follow the coastline and hide in the forest.

Unfortunately, though the beach contained a few broken tree trunks and branches, nothing seemed large enough to hide him from their view. And he thought crawling would be too slow to stay out of their reach.

A noise came from behind him, startling him out of his thoughts. A finned doll breached the shore, its silvery body shining in the green sunlight.

Bekk knew the creatures were friendly, as he'd met one before, but without Ryf here to speak to it in its own language, Bekk decided to give it a wide berth. He didn't want to inadvertently provoke the thing.

The finned doll let out a quiet, mournful sound, like a low brass instrument.

Bekk ignored it, refocusing on his path to flee.

The creature sidled up onto the sand, reached out with a fin, and slapped Bekk gently on the foot.

"What the...?" Bekk said, glancing down at it.

The finned doll turned, so its head faced the water. It then peered at Bekk and made the same sound.

"I'm sorry," he said, knowing the creature wouldn't understand. "I can't help you. And Ryf isn't here."

Bekk began to crawl to the end of the fallen tree, ready to move as fast as he could along the beach, the air in his lungs moving in and out with adrenaline-fueled speed.

The finned doll followed, burrowing quickly through the sand, faster than Bekk had moved, and caught up to him. He slapped Bekk's foot again, this time a little harder.

"What?" Bekk snapped, pulling his foot away.

The finned doll once more faced the Eclipse Sea, glanced over its shoulder at Bekk, and wailed softly.

"I can't follow you," Bekk said, trying to determine the creature's meaning. "I can't breathe underwater." Bekk paused. Or could he? The rules of Iyah were different than on Earth. He didn't need to eat or sleep here. He felt cold and hot, but never sick. Was he even breathing oxygen right now? Could he perhaps breathe underwater, too?

The finned doll slapped its flipper against the sand and wiggled towards the water, then stared once again at Bekk.

Bekk's mind whirled. *Okay,* he thought. *Even if I can't breathe underwater, swimming down the coastline may actually be better. It'll keep me hidden long enough to put sufficient distance from the soldiers until I can get onto land again and run.*

"All right," he said, scuttling along. He sidled up next to the finned doll. "Lead the way."

The finned doll moaned again, then slapped Bekk on the hand.

"What?" Bekk said, not understanding.

The creature slapped his hand again and then wiggled its back.

Bekk paused. "Are you serious?"

Another wiggle.

Bekk reached out gingerly, ready to remove his hand in case he'd misinterpreted the creature, and wrapped his fingertips around the top edge of its curved shoulder joint. He expected it to feel slick or slimy, but instead it felt more like fine sandpaper, and his grip seemed secure.

The finned doll let out a short, low blow and suddenly took off.

Bekk's fingers curled, tightening his grip. The water's edge rushed towards them and suddenly he was plunged beneath the lavender waves.

The coolness of the water felt good against his sun-heated face, but the shock to the rest of his body caused him to tighten up for several moments. The finned doll remained close to the surface, heading a bit out to sea, before it stopped.

Moment of truth, Bekk thought. He stuck his head underwater and inhaled.

Big mistake!

Bekk's head popped up above the surface, coughing intensely as the water he'd breathed in shot out from his lungs. After heaving in a few deep breaths, he shook the excess moisture from his eyes and treaded water. *Well, that solves* that *question.*

Still, swimming seemed like the best option. He could move down the coastline a bit and then reemerge when he felt safe.

Something touched him underwater. Bekk ducked below the surface. The finned doll appeared to be waiting to help him, but Bekk didn't know if he should take the creature's help. It may swim further out to sea or even worse, down towards the bottom.

Bekk wished Ryf was there to translate. How could he tell the creature he didn't need its help anymore?

A strange sound floated through Bekk's head. It sounded like the finned doll's moaning, but...Bekk could understand it!

Down, you can hear me. Up, I can hear you. Work together. Swim together. Save the throne.

Bekk ran out of air and resurfaced. The finned doll's head did as well.

"Ryf told me you couldn't understand me," he told it. They both resubmerged.

You were not of here. I did not trust at start. Ryf is friend and trusts with you. I learned what you voiced, to understand.

They both came up again. "Well, that's good to hear. At least I have someone to talk to. Do you know what's going on at the castle?

Can you help bring me south," Bekk said, pointing with his left hand, "down the coastline?"

Under once more.

Yes. Each realm feels the throne. It is not ours anymore. It is changing things. Iyah is coming together. But the throne cannot fix itself. It is not useful without passage. It will become the after-Iyah place. Come, grab hold. We will swim.

Bekk's head popped up above the water, gasping for air. He'd waited to hear everything the finned doll had said, but it pushed his lungs to capacity. Not everything made sense to him, but at least he had transportation. Bekk once again wrapped his fingers around the edge of the creature's shell and hung on.

Just before they were about to take off, Bekk glanced at the beach. The green soldiers were in sight now, but it didn't seem as though they'd spotted him in the water. A breath of relief gushed out of him.

Suddenly, two figures appeared on the sand, out of nowhere.

The figures were *not* made of stone.

Though a little way out, Bekk recognized them instantly: Belle and Vic.

Oh no!

The Jade soldiers pointed in his friends' direction, running towards them. Bekk frantically splashed, yelling out to them.

"Over here!" he screamed. "In the water!"

Vic must have heard him because he grabbed Belle's hand and dragged her towards the water's edge. The two of them hit the water in a sprint, hurdling over the smaller waves near the shore, Vic's long legs managing the task more easily. Vic finally dove headfirst into an oncoming wave. When his head surfaced, he ended up about halfway between the water's edge and Bekk.

"Vic!" Bekk called out, swimming over to his friend.

Vic was ignoring Bekk, staring instead at the shore. "Belle!!" he hollered. The two of them watched as Belle floundered in the pounding surf. A head shorter than Vic and less streamlined, she hadn't been able to run as quickly, and her clothing—flannel pajamas—was wet and bogging her down.

"Oh my God, Belle!" Vic began to swim towards the beach. The finned doll left Bekk's side. He thought it was going to go and retrieve Belle, but instead it swam directly in front of Vic, stopping his path.

"What the hell is this thing? Get out of my way!" Vic screeched, shoving at the creature.

Bekk realized the truth. The stone soldiers *did* move faster than humans. In that short time span they'd already crossed the distance to the beach's edge and were dragging Belle across the sand. The finned doll must have understood that Vic would never reach her in time.

"Vic, VIC!" Bekk cried out. His arms and legs felt wobbly from treading water. He managed to paddle his way over to his friend, who still wrestled with the finned doll. "It's too late, Vic. They have her. Stop struggling and listen to me!"

Vic stopped, fury on his face when he turned towards Bekk.

Bekk saw the finned doll's head above water. "Can you float between us? We need something to hold on to."

The creature complied, bobbing gently between the two of them. Bekk gestured for Vic to grab hold of the finned doll, which he finally did.

"Why did you stop me? Why didn't you wait for us on the beach?" Vic asked, his eyes bulging in their sockets. Water dripped off his afro-puffed hair, beading down his face.

"I didn't know you two were going to show up," Bekk said in a defensive tone. The reality finally sunk in and he shivered. "Besides, you couldn't have helped her. They would have taken you, too."

"At least she wouldn't be alone."

"Then we'll get her back. But we need a plan first." He nudged Vic's shoulder and his friend pulled his gaze from the shoreline. "If we are going to get her away from them, I'll need your help."

Vic didn't reply, his face tight with concern and anger.

Bekk figured that was the best response he'd get for right now. He tapped on the finned doll and it lifted its head. "Let's head south. Not too fast."

The finned doll began to swim. Vic's eyes widened, but he held on. The creature moved them down the coastline, while Vic's gaze returned and remained locked securely on the last place he'd seen Belle until they'd moved far enough away for it to be out of sight.

"I'm sure she'll be okay," Bekk said, having no idea if his words held any truth. "Besides, you two never stay here for long. She'll probably wake up before they even get all the way to the castle."

Vic shook his head. "You don't understand."

Bekk kept one eye on the coastline. He'd have the finned doll swim them around the area where the firestream deposited into the sea. At that point, they'd be close enough to find shelter in the Sunbeam Forest.

"What don't I understand?" He paused, suddenly realizing something. "And where's Ashlee? Didn't she come with you again?"

"Bekk, listen."

Bekk turned his full attention towards his friend. "What is it?"

Vic's face looked haggard, as if he'd been up cramming for a final. "It's been one day since we were here last."

"It's been two days here. You know time is different."

"That's not what I'm talking about."

Bekk frowned. "What, then?"

Vic waited a few moments to respond as a small purplish wave struck him in the face. He sputtered, then continued. "You know how Ashlee didn't come with us the last time to Iyah, when we showed up outside the castle and you said the Jade King had taken it over? Well, when Belle and I woke up after that visit, Ashlee didn't wake up."

"What do you mean? I figured she never fell asleep with you and Belle."

"Well she did. And she didn't...wake...up."

The words finally struck Bekk. A sinking sensation flooded his body. He tapped on the finned doll so it would stop, to fully focus on Vic's words. "What do you mean?"

"I mean, she's in a coma. She won't wake up, man. She's in the hospital."

Bekk felt like he might burst apart. "A coma?"

"Yeah."

Bekk remembered the time he'd been in a coma, at the end of the school year. At that time, Ryf had "brought" Bekk to Iyah and kept him here against his will. Because of that, his body on Earth had shut down and stayed "asleep" in a coma. He'd been in the hospital for three days. "But she's not in Iyah. That doesn't make sense. Why isn't she waking up?"

"I don't know, Bekk, but it freaked the hell out of us. We had to have the maid call her parents, who were out of town for the weekend and didn't even know we were staying over. We remained with her at the hospital until her parents showed up. They were furious. They blamed us, saying we probably did drugs or were goofing around and she fell or something. They wouldn't let us stay."

Vic shook his head and continued. "What could we do? We couldn't tell them 'oh no, it's fine, she's just stuck in a dream world.' They'd think we were insane." Vic paused and averted his eyes. "Look, I'll be honest. I didn't want to come here again for her, but Belle insisted. She said you'd know how to wake Ashlee up. She was so insistent, she snuck over to my house to sleep. She figured we couldn't come here unless we were together because we weren't able to come separately before."

"Oh, God," Bekk said. He shivered, but this time it wasn't just from disbelief. The water temperature was dropping as the sun lowered in the sky. He tapped the finned doll and it continued on. At the rate they were moving, it should only take a few more minutes before they reached their destination.

Sure enough, Bekk could see where the firestream churned into the water. Heaps of steam floated above the area and several water creatures bathed and frolicked where the heat met the sea.

Bekk tapped on the finned doll. "There," he said, pointing just past the firestream's exit point. The creature sped them along, moving around the region of streaming water, and within moments they were on the beach again.

The two of them crawled onto the sand, their clothing soaked. Vic lay, panting, face up. Bekk made himself sit up.

"We have to keep moving," Bekk said. "Into the forest. It's just a few hundred feet away."

"No," Vic said.

Bekk hesitated. "No?"

"No. I'm going to lay here until I wake up. And then I'm going to wake up Belle to get her away from those soldiers. I shouldn't have let Belle convince me to return here. I don't care about this place anymore. I'm sorry, man, but I want to go home. I want to know Belle's okay."

"I told you, you don't stay long. I'm sure you'll wake up soon, but you can't stay on this beach. It's too exposed."

Vic's eyes widened as he stared into the sky. He kept talking, as if he didn't care what Bekk had just said. "What if she doesn't wake up?" Vic turned his face towards Bekk. "What if she ends up like Ashlee? You didn't see her, Bekk. We shook her and yelled at her and she didn't wake up. She's stuck, wherever she is. I'm scared for her. I'm scared for Belle. And I'm scared for me. I'm sorry you can't leave this place, but I don't want to be lost here, too. And now Belle might be trapped here with some crazy stone people? Uh uh. I'm done." He faced the sky once more. "If they find me, at least they'll take me to Belle. I shouldn't have left her on that beach..."

Bekk wasn't sure what to say. Mixed emotions sifted through him. Guilt sprung to the forefront—guilt that he'd somehow brought his friends here in the first place. Now Belle was captured by the soldiers and Ashlee lay in a coma...

What's going on? he thought. *Why isn't Ashlee waking up? Did she get caught in Iyah somewhere? But that doesn't make sense. No matter what was ever happening to me, I could always wake up eventually. Even when Ryf brought me here, I decided to leave and I could. The only time I didn't wake up was when I decided to stay, to keep my brother out.*

Is that what happened to Ashlee? Did she somehow choose to stay? If so, then why is her body in a coma and not dead?

Too many unanswered questions. As much as Ashlee's whereabouts flittered through his mind, there was nothing he could do about her right now. What he could do was help his friend and find Belle.

"Vic, I get it. And I'm sorry. I really am. I never thought any of you would come here to find me. Once you did get here, I never thought about the consequences. I was so happy to see you I didn't think that anything could go wrong."

Vic lay still for a few beats, still staring at the sky. Finally, his mouth released a long sigh.

"It's not your fault, man. You didn't ask us to come here. You didn't even know we *could* come here. I just..." He sat up and gazed out across the Eclipse Sea. "I thought this was so maxxed, finding out this place was real, finding out you were still alive. Well, kind of alive."

Bekk gave a weak grin, but let his friend continue.

"But I didn't take this place seriously. I still thought of it like a dream. And..." Vic trailed off, hanging his head.

"What?" Bekk prompted.

"I thought it would help me finish my game."

It took Bekk a few moments to figure out what Vic meant. Then he remembered. Vic had been creating a video game based off Bekk's descriptions of Iyah.

"You're still working on that?" Bekk asked.

Vic nodded. "Yeah. But I'm stuck at the ending, about the castle. You never told me what it looked like, on the inside at least. And then I started feeling like a fraud. I hadn't *made up* the game at all. I only used what you told me about it." Vic let out a grunt and stood, brusquely trying to brush the sand from his wet clothes.

"I took for granted that Ashlee would wake up eventually. It wasn't until Belle told me at the end of the day that she hadn't that I started to worry about this place. I started to feel like...like I never came here to help you. That I only came here to finish my game. That I didn't think of it as real and now Ashlee is stuck here and Belle got taken..." Vic picked up a piece of driftwood and chucked it into the water.

Bekk stood next to his friend. He didn't have any words of comfort. What could he say? He couldn't reprimand Vic for his intentions. This place was *supposed* to feel like a safe haven. It had been designed that way. Why wouldn't Vic think he and the girls could just pop in and out whenever they wanted, like an adventure in a story, helping when they could without any repercussions?

"This place," Bekk finally said. "isn't a bad place. Normally. It's supposed to help people. But it's in trouble, and it's not working like it's supposed to." Bekk exhaled and continued. "I thought my brother was the problem. I thought I'd fixed everything. But I had no idea what was really going on. As for Shon...I didn't realize how tough things were for him. He was so busy taking care of me after our parents died...but he didn't have anyone to help him."

"That's not your fault."

"Maybe not, but I still feel responsible. We only had the two of us. I should have been more aware."

Vic faced Bekk. "You don't know *what* might have happened differently. My mom always says 'should'a's are just someone's way of guilting themselves into doing something.' It comes from regret or fear, not truth."

A moment of silence.

"That's deep, man," Bekk said, cracking a grin.

Vic smiled and let out a snort. "Seriously, though, your brother made his own choices. And you gave up your life to stop him." He turned away again. "And I came here to learn about a castle for a game."

"Vic, I don't believe that. And I don't think you do either. It took me months to realize Iyah was real. I treated it like it was just in my head. Ryf's friend, Yir, gave up her life to save me. My brother was killing fairies. Some guy made out of rock is threatening this place... and I don't really know what the hell I'm doing. Now my girlfriend is in a coma and my longest-known friend is kept in some castle with huge stone soldiers." Bekk kicked at the sand. "I hate it here sometimes."

"But you said it helped you, as a kid."

"It did. A lot. And it helped Ashlee, too. I mean, it must have if she came here when she was younger."

Vic ran his hand over his afro. "I'm scared we aren't going to find the girls."

Bekk felt his own doubt rolling through his stomach. "I'm sure this is the part where I'm supposed to give some sort of motivational speech, you know, like in the movies, but I've got nothing. All I can say is, I'm going to do everything I can to help Belle and find out what happened to Ashlee. I just don't have any idea how."

"Do you think we can?"

"I've got no clue. All I know is I can't leave this place, so I'm going to do whatever it takes to survive and stop those stone soldiers." Bekk paused. "I'd like you to come with and help, but that's the tricky thing about Iyah. It can put you where you need to be, but it can't make you do anything. It has to be your choice." Bekk could feel the lump in his throat as he waited for Vic to make his decision.

With a grunt, Vic turned away from the sea. "Well, I suppose the first step is for us to find some cover in the forest. Then, we figure out a way to take down these stone jerks."

Relief washed over Bekk. "I like the way you think. Let's go."

CHAPTER 7

The Jade King stared down at the smaller pinkish creature. She was much too large to be a fairy. She appeared more like the shape of the puppet, Shon, which the Jade King previously controlled, feeding him jade to harden him, manipulating him to keep the archway open.

But the Jade King didn't realize more of these beings existed in Iyah. He'd only learned about fairies from his puppet. He'd never been told there were more of these squishy things. She had been brought here by his guards, not a fairy, no, but still an excellent find.

The creature itself, however, was belligerent, loud, and uncooperative.

"I will ask again," the Jade King said, his tone threatening. "Where can I find the fairies?"

"And I will tell you again," she replied, arms crossed. "I. Don't. Know. But even if I did, I wouldn't tell you."

The Jade King ground his jaw. Normally, he'd place her in his dungeons, give her time to *want* to talk. The problem revolved around the fact that this castle didn't belong to him. He didn't even know if it *had* a dungeon. The only room he could visit was the bedroom on the same floor as the throne room, where the arch had appeared, because when he attempted to go down the stairs to the entranceway...

A shudder rippled through him at the memory of so many overlapping doors. He didn't know how to control them, or how to access them. He'd been confused and dizzy and immediately returned to the throne room, to touch the throne and absorb its energy until he regained his stability.

The Jade King decided a different tactic might work—to use the pearly substance on her, but after he *tried,* he discovered she wouldn't succumb to the pearly substance like his guards. She maintained her own free will. He wondered if that meant she were powerful in some way foreign to him so she could deflect his control. If she had power, he wanted to harness it.

And lastly, though he didn't want to admit it even to himself, he found himself enjoying the company of another sentient being. The isolation drained him. Perhaps a conversation could be used to his advantage.

"We are at an impasse," he said, switching gears to diplomacy.

"Not if you let me go."

"Go? Go where? To the fairies? Or others of your kind? My guards told me how distant the water lay from this castle, how they mostly carried you as they ran. Do you expect to trudge across the plains on your own?" He nodded at the windows surrounding the room. "The sun will fall soon. I will admit, I do not know everything about this realm. I do not know the safety of the night. Do you?"

Though she didn't answer, the Jade King was adept at reading body language. The slight shuffle of her feet, the pursing of her mouth, the glance at the setting sun through the windows all indicated her uncertainty.

The Jade King paused in thought. Perhaps this creature was as lost as he was? Perhaps a different tactic would work better.

"I suggest you be my guest tonight in the castle. Once the sun rises, I will release you."

Her eyes widened. "You will?"

"Yes. I do not wish to antagonize those who live in this realm."

"Oh, I don't live here."

The Jade King stored this information in his mind. If she didn't live here, then she must come from another place. And if that were the case, then perhaps he could learn how she traveled between worlds.

"This is also not my home," he told her.

She snorted. "I know. You don't exactly fit in with the concept of fairies."

"True. But I do *fit* here."

Her forehead wrinkled. "What do you mean?"

The Jade King gestured to the chair in which he sat. "This throne, does it look like it would fit a fairy?"

A peek at the large chair. "Well...no. But I assumed you brought it with you from whatever world you came from."

"I did not. It was here when I arrived. Even for you, who does not appear as a fairy either, would feel a bit small sitting on it, correct?"

"I guess so."

"Why would there be a throne here that is made for someone like me if I am not meant to sit in it?"

Silence.

The Jade King resisted smiling.

"I just know you aren't supposed to be here," she said.

"How do you know that?"

"My friends told me."

"The fairies would want to keep this castle to themselves, even if it isn't made for them."

"Just because there is one throne that's too big..."

The Jade King stood abruptly, a smirk touching his mouth at seeing the girl startled. "If you'd follow me?" He strode away without a glance at her, knowing she'd follow. He took brisk steps, content that his strength had almost fully returned, and arrived at the room which had contained the arch. He entered. Sure enough, lagging only a bit behind, she caught up to him.

"This is a bedroom. You can see the bed. Does that look like it is made for a fairy? Or even for you?"

The girl said nothing, her stare slowly circling the room.

"I believe I belong here in this kingdom, but the fairies will not help me. If you know them, perhaps you can tell them of my intent and hospitality. So, this is where you'll stay for the evening," he told her. "But before you retire, I hope we can converse more. You see," he said, nodding to the wall, "that is where I entered. The archway that led me here has disappeared. I cannot return home." He waited patiently as she moved around the room, her fingertips trailing lightly on the wall where the arch had been.

"Why did you come here?" she finally asked.

The Jade King took a moment to answer. Though his body had regained most of its strength, he still sensed a weariness inside himself. He'd been pursuing this goal for 3,000 years and the finality of the situation weighed upon him.

"I was...shown...that I would come here," he began, taking a seat in a chair in the corner of the room by the door. "To save my people." The words came, though he didn't know why he felt compelled to tell her. Perhaps he needed her to understand. Perhaps he only missed the company of another. "There was a war, and my people suffered. I have done all I can, but it isn't enough. We are not recovering. We are not going to survive. Three thousand years I've been trying to restore my land and it still isn't enough time."

"How can comin' here save them?"

"There is a resource I need, a type of resin. It has many helpful properties and is necessary for construction, health...so many things. The war divided the land and we were cut off from the supply of resin we needed. I was told that if I came here, I could access other worlds which have that resin, and bring it home to my people."

The girl sat on the edge of the bed, listening, but still taut. "Then why do you need a fairy?"

"They are the only ones who can open a door to those other worlds."

She shook her head. "You want to kill them to do it. I've heard about you and what you've done. And who's to say you won't just plunder another world, take their 'resin' or whatever and leave them high and dry?"

Anger flared up inside him. He believed it rose because of her insolence, but it surprised him. He was angry with himself. This girl, this *nothing* creature, was right. He *would* do those things. He'd do anything to save his people.

It had been so long since he'd taken counsel with anyone about his plans. Even those he spoke to in the past—his children, his Love, his closest court members—never knew his true desires. And he knew, now, why. He knew they saw him as this girl looked at him now. With shame, disgust, even pity. He'd never told anyone because he knew his idea was monstrous.

And to be a savior, he needed to be a monster.

"I..." he started. "I want to save my people."

"At the cost of your soul?"

The girl's words cut deep.

Before he could respond, as if she'd never even been there, the girl vanished.

CHAPTER 8

"A grim-shu?" Jayla exclaimed, a shiver running through her. "I'm going to become that transparent, monstrous, soulless, *thing*!?" She stroked her arms, as if sure at any moment they would become intangible.

The Basalt woman continued to usher her inside the house and steered her toward the kitchen table. Simply made from limestone, it stood low and sturdy, clearly able to hold up the mountains of food being prepared in the kitchen. Scents and smells wafted across the room, but they only made Jayla nauseous as fear spiked in her belly. The idea of turning into that slithering creature that had hunted her in the Onyx Mountains turned her insides cold.

"Don't worry, dear, nothing is going to 'appen to you just yet. You've got four, maybe five days or so before any changes start."

"A few days? That's not really reassuring," Jayla muttered. The woman placed a bowl of something steaming in front of her. It looked a bit like iron chunks in some sort of limestone sauce. Jayla ignored it as her stomach fought between hunger and panic.

How could things have gotten so out of control? she wondered.

Just a week ago, everything had been normal. She'd been in Jade Castle, celebrating her father's Metamorph Day with him and her brother. They'd been happy and safe.

And now...

Now, her brother lay dead, killed by her father's hand. Afterwards, she'd fled the castle because she'd once told a story that foretold a scenario in which her father would keep her captive, a story she believed because a few random strangers told her she had the power of foresight as an oracle. She now stood in the Basalt Territory, knowing no one, about to turn into a creature of the mountains. A creature she'd never even heard of a week ago.

The hugeness of these changes threatened to swallow her whole. A heaviness settled in her chest, a darkness in her mind.

It would be easier to hide. Be on your own. Stay in the mountains. Leave this pain behind.

Jayla's eyelids snapped open. She hadn't even realized she'd closed them. Those thoughts. They didn't really feel like her, even though they existed in her mind.

The grim-shu is already trying to take over, she thought with a shudder.

"Chilly, dear?" the woman asked.

"Not really. Thank you." Jayla pushed the bowl away. The smell didn't entice her anymore. The rocks were old, dead. It wasn't what she wanted.

Something fresher. More...alive.

"Stop it!" Jayla said out loud.

"Sorry," the woman said, retreating.

"Not you," Jayla told her, tears in her eyes. She took in a shuddering breath. "What happens during the transformation? And is there any way to stop it?"

The woman gave a smile. "Of course, dear. Not to worry."

Relief like a lava wave flooded over her. "Oh good. What's the cure?"

"There's a type of crystal, formed where the Pearl River empties into the Lava Circle. It just needs to be ground up and ingested."

"Well that doesn't sound so bad."

Basala snorted from the corner. "These Jade-folk. They don't know nothing."

"'Ush," the woman said, shushing him.

"What don't I know?" Jayla asked.

The woman placed a drink on the table as well. "The crystals ain't easy to get to, dear, that's all. But there's a tiny town, not much more than a speck, 'bout a day away, where they collect and sell them. We'll purchase what we need there."

Jayla thought about the coins and jewelry she'd taken when she escaped the Jade Castle. She could have sold them to purchase her cure, but she'd lost them when the grim-shu snatched away her bag. "I-I don't have any way to pay for the crystals," Jayla said, stuttering. Another chill raced through her at the thought that she would have no choice but to become a grim-shu.

"Don't choo worry," the woman said. "We will cover the cost."

"We will?" Basala said.

"Yes," she said, glaring at him. "You know she's important to

Basaila."

Surprise hit Jayla. "Wait, I thought *you* were Basaila."

"Me?" the woman said with a soft laugh. "Oh no, not me. Basaila is a Roamer. She should be 'ere soon. She knew you'd come."

"What's a Roamer?"

Basala let out a grunt, threw up his hands, and exited the house.

The woman pursed her lips at his retreating figure. "Don't mind 'im. 'E forgets that the people of each land have been separated for too long. Our words, our customs, even our resources 'ave changed. I'm sure they 'ave for the Jade folk as well. It's just been too long, for all."

She shook her head slightly, as if bringing herself out of her reverie. "Any'oo, dear, a Roamer is someone 'oo 'as no 'ome, but is welcome in any 'ome. They often spread news from other towns or bring 'elp or supplies if needed. And, once in a great while, they are an oracle, like Basaila."

A flitter of excitement entered Jayla's chest. "Can she really see the future?" She'd been told that her gift lay inside the stories she told. Stories she thought she'd made up, but apparently, she was simply speaking of things that had happened or would happen to others.

"Oh yes. But it ain't no parlor trick. She's not a conjurer on a whim, dear. 'Er visions take a lot of concentration and time. They don't come to 'er out of nowhere."

A frown touched Jayla's lips. That didn't sound the same as what happened to her. She never had to try. The words simply flowed from her mouth, as if someone else supplied them.

Stories are for the weak. Strength will keep you going. Eat and I will make you strong.

Jayla shook her head at the intruding thoughts. "I don't mean to be rude—you've already done so much for me—but...this business about turning into a grim-shu. Should I be worried about the voice in my head?"

The woman paled, her dark skin turning a strange grayish-green color. "You...you 'ear a voice?"

"Yes. I think...I think it is the grim-shu. At least, they are not things I would normally think."

"Is it telling you to eat? Telling you to find strength?"

"Yes."

The woman began to pace. "Oh, dear. Oh, dear me," she murmured.

"Is that a problem?" Anxiety shot through Jayla's body.

"Well, now, there's no need to worry, per se. It's just...that symptom usually don't 'appen until close to when you're gonna change."

The panic exploded inside Jayla's chest, constricting it. Her breaths came quicker and she clasped her hands over her heart as if to protect it. "What does that mean?"

"Nothing. All it means is we can't wait for Basaila to return. I was going to send Basala to fetch the crystals for you 'ere, but that'll take too long. You'll 'ave to travel with 'im to Bagem Market. I fear in the time for 'im to go there and back, it'll be too late. But if you go with 'im, yes, yes that'll be in plenty of time."

Jayla knew the woman meant to reassure her, but the concern

in her voice was obvious.

At that moment, Basala reentered, carrying a large chunk of some dark stone in his arms.

"Good timing," the woman said. "You will 'ave to leave for Bagem tonight. With the girl."

Basala eyed Jayla. "I was planning on going in the morn. I 'ave chores to take care of."

"I know, but the timetable is...faster than normal. She won't make it for the two to three days it normally takes for a round trip."

Jayla didn't feel all that comfortable traveling with this man who didn't seem to have much interest in her wellbeing. "Perhaps I can go on my own, if you can give me directions? I don't want to be a burden."

"There's that word again," the woman said. "Not a burden. Promise. Basala just forgets 'imself. And why we do what we do."

A brief tension filled the room as the woman stared at Basala. He almost seemed as though he wanted to resist, but then Jayla watched as his shoulders relaxed. He nodded his head. "I know," he said. "It's just been a lot o' years."

"The time is almost up," the woman said, a strength in her voice.

Basala nodded again then turned towards Jayla. "I'll meet you outside when you're ready. We'll take mokaki mounts, to be on the safe side." He left the house.

Mokaki are also tasty, though they squirm.

Jayla felt sick to her stomach at the thought in her head. "I can't thank you enough," Jayla said, forcing herself to ignore the voice.

"Basala, too."

The woman wrapped Jayla into a hug. The motion felt almost foreign to Jayla, who hadn't received such an embrace since her mother had been alive over a century ago.

"You are special, dear," the woman said. "You will do great things." She released Jayla and held her at arm's length, peering into her eyes. "Listen closely to my words. We 'ave lost people to the grim-shu, but it is few and far between now. Basala will keep you safe. Stay near 'im. 'E knows what to do with the crystals, but just in case something 'appens, I'll tell you what to do, too. You will 'ave to buy three, about the length of your fingers. They will need to be grinded down into a fine powder. Once this 'appens, the powder must be mixed with a limestone paste and consumed within two 'ours of the grinding, otherwise the potency will be gone. You must accomplish this when you are yourself, before you turn into a grim-shu."

The woman released Jayla's arms, but the intensity remained in her eyes. "The grim-shu's call is very strong. It will tempt you. As you become more like it, you'll feel your own voice is the stranger in your 'ead, not the other way around. Basala will stay with you when you change. When the grim-shu takes you over fully, Basala will 'elp you see your reflection. 'E's got plenty of time to do this—over eight 'ours before you won't no longer be you ever again. When you see your own face, though, it will remind you that you are *not* really a grim-shu, since they are only representations of our former selves. When you see your reflection, *'old onto the thought of you.* Then, you'll be in your own mind and return to yourself."

Fear still clenched Jayla's chest, but she forced in a deep breath. "I understand."

Jayla headed towards the rear door.

"One more thing, dear," the woman added.

"Yes?"

"Basaila will be 'ere when you return. She will 'ave answers to your questions. When you're done, 'urry back."

"I will. I promise. Thank you again." Jayla gave a genuine smile, then turned away, her body rigid with determination.

You will become me.

Yes, Jayla thought at the voice as she exited the house into the cool air outside, *but I will return as myself. I will find out who I am from Basaila, and learn the next step on my path.*

We shall see...

CHAPTER 9

"Shon, you have visitors."

Adrenaline shot through him. It was Ashlee, Vic, and Belle. He knew it. They hadn't come yesterday like they said they would, but they'd shown up today.

"I'll be right there," he replied with a smile. "Need to use the bathroom first."

"I'll let them know." The nurse paused and smiled. "I'll bet they'll be excited to hear you're going to be released soon."

"Yeah. Can't wait to tell them," Shon lied. Truth was, he wasn't sure he wanted to tell anyone yet. After his few visits from Bekk's friends, he'd apparently shown improvement to the doctors. His main psychiatrist, Dr. Nancy Romal, said she'd been impressed with his change in attitude.

"What's different?" she'd asked, removing and polishing her glasses on a white handkerchief she pulled out of her blazer pocket.

"I don't know," he said slowly. "I guess...after seeing my brother's friends, I felt different. Like...a weight had been lifted off me. They made me remember my brother, not just that he died, you know?"

"Well I have to say, it's wonderful to see it. In fact, if you keep feeling this good, we may be able look at reinstating you in the world again. Would you like that?"

Shon had responded with an affirmative, but truthfully, he wasn't sure. He'd been convinced he should stay locked up, especially for his part in Bekk's death, but now? Maybe he could help Bekk through his friends. And relying on visiting hours wasn't the easiest way to do that.

Shon shook himself from his thoughts and watched the nurse glide from his room, her flats silent on the carpeted floor. As soon as she'd gone, Shon raced to the bathroom and wiggled the loose tile. He pulled out the pages he'd drafted about Iyah and shoved them down the back of his pants. With a deep breath to slow his racing heart, he headed towards the visitor's area.

When he entered, the first thing he noticed was that the blonde girl, Ashlee, wasn't with the other two.

"Hey," he said, taking a seat across from them. "I was hoping to hear from you again yesterday. How did things go Friday night?"

The two exchanged a look.

"What?" Shon asked. "What's wrong?"

"It's about Ashlee," Belle said, a catch in her words.

Concern crept into Shon's chest. "What about her?"

"Maybe we should start from the beginning," Vic suggested. He glanced at Shon. "A lot has happened."

Shon shifted in his seat, his hands sweaty. "Is she okay? Is Bekk all right?"

"Wait, man," Vic said, holding up a hand. "Let Belle tell you."

The concern slid into worry, but Shon kept his mouth shut. He hadn't always been the most patient person, resulting in a quick temper and more fights than he cared to admit. Besides, one of those fights was the reason his parents died in the first place. But he'd worked hard, after his parents' car accident, to get his impatience under control. He didn't want his temper to be the cause of pain for anyone else.

"Okay. Go ahead."

Belle launched into the story about how Friday night they'd all fallen asleep at Ashlee's house, how they'd met up with Bekk in Iyah, except that Ashlee wasn't with them.

"Did she maybe not fall asleep?" Shon interrupted.

"Hold on," Vic said.

"Sorry, sorry."

"Anyway," Belle continued, "when Vic and I got there, we met Bekk outside the castle. He was on the run, with a ton of fairies. Apparently, that Jade King you were talkin' about before? He came in and conquered the castle, turned some throne into jade rock, so Bekk and the fairies had to flee."

Shon gripped the edge of the table, but kept his mouth shut, knowing that there was more to the story.

"After that," she went on, "we all ran to the beach. When we got there, though, Vic and I woke up. It was then Saturday mornin', well, yesterday mornin'. Except Ashlee wouldn't wake up. She's..." Belle paused, swallowing hard. "She's in a coma."

Wheels spun in Shon's mind. "Like what happened to Bekk at

the end of the school year," he muttered. "He couldn't return from Iyah, so his body stayed asleep here."

"That's what we figured, too," Belle said. "Except...," she looked at Vic.

"Except we don't know where she is in Iyah, since she wasn't with us," Vic finished.

"We told her parents, who of course freaked out, and came home early from their business trip. They wouldn't let us see her in the hospital yesterday. I think they believe it's our fault, angry that we stayed over while they were out of town. But I kept callin' them and they finally gave in and let us visit this mornin'."

"Is she still in the hospital?" Shon asked.

Belle nodded. "We checked in on her before we came here. No change."

Shon slumped in his chair. Another kid, hurt in this world because of Iyah. This was all his fault. If it weren't for him, Bekk wouldn't have been brought to Iyah by the fairies in the first place and then Bekk's friends wouldn't have gotten involved.

Vic spoke up next. "Belle insisted we try to go back to Iyah last night, to find Ashlee. I snuck over to her house and slept on the floor because we knew we couldn't get to Iyah by ourselves."

"I take it you didn't have any luck finding her?" Shon said, defeat in his tone.

Belle shook her head. "If she's there, we don't know where she is, and neither did any of the fairies. But somethin' else happened."

"What?" Shon asked, preparing for more bad news.

"I got kidnapped by some Jade soldiers and spoke with the Jade

King," Belle answered.

That got Shon's attention. "You were with him? Inside Yar Castle?"

"Yep. His guards caught me on the beach and marched me to the castle. Well, basically carried me. They can move so fast. Anyway, when I got there, I walked into this room, where there were like a million doors, and I felt really dizzy. The guards just kept movin' and somehow we were on some stairs and then at another door. Once in there, the room seemed fine, though huge, with like a hundred more soldiers and the Jade King sittin' on a large, green throne."

Shon recognized her description of the entrance to Yar Castle with the overlapping doors and entrances. The guards must have figured out how to make the room work, but the doors should have gone away once they moved through the room with their destination locked in their minds. Could something else be moving them through the castle without them having to think?

"At that point," Vic said, pulling Shon from his thoughts, "we got woken up by Belle's mom, who'd knocked on the door and peeked in to wake her up. Luckily, she didn't come in all the way and catch me, since I slept on the far side of the room out of sight on the floor next to Belle's bed." Vic scooted his chair closer to Belle and put an arm around her. "I was so scared for you with those soldiers," he said. She tipped her head against his shoulder.

A feeling of both warmth and bitterness coursed through Shon's body. He remembered that sensation of trust and caring. The memory felt like it belonged to someone else.

Shon cleared his throat and the two of them pulled themselves from their moment of closeness.

"Listen..." he began slowly. "Maybe you two shouldn't deal with Iyah anymore. You've been lucky so far, but things that happen there affect this reality. I hate to say this, but Ashlee might never wake up. Bekk's already gone. You two should think about your futures."

"I won't leave Ashlee there," Belle said, her eyes narrow. "I don't care about the risk. And this Jade King guy? I met him. He may be horrible, but there's somethin' about him. I think he wants to believe he is doing all this for a good reason. If we can talk to him some more, convince him to stop, maybe he'll restore the castle."

Shon shook his head. "You don't know him like I do. He's...determined. Single-minded."

"Maybe. But I also know he seemed to be at a loss. I think his goal was to get into Iyah, but now that he's there, he can't move forward. He's stuck. And he has all these guards with them, but they just stand there, unmovin', unless he orders them to do somethin'. They don't talk or move or blink or *anythin'*. He doesn't have anyone to help him. He's cut off from home."

Shon thought about it. Memories of what the Jade King had done to manipulate him, to help him feel less compassion, encourage him to destroy the fairies for Shon's own personal gain...

"He's dangerous," he said, still not convinced. "If he thinks you can help him achieve his goal, he'll use you, even if you die." Shon remembered the feeling of removing the life force from the fairies in order to cross through the open doors to other worlds. The jade which infected him made him care less, but a part of him still felt revulsion each time. He turned towards Vic, forcing himself away from his dark thoughts. "What about you? Do you want to return?"

Vic squirmed in his seat, not answering right away, and Belle looked at him, confusion in her eyes.

"Not really," he said softly.

Belle's mouth dropped open.

"I'm sorry," he said to her, "but it's the truth. When I saw you getting taken away by those guards, I nearly lost my mind. I didn't know what had happened to you, if I'd wake up the next morning and find you in a coma, or worse, dead!" He turned his face away. Shon could see him fighting to keep his emotions under control.

Belle said nothing. She simply swiveled her body to face Shon again, her head hanging a bit.

Shon cleared his throat again. "Look, I'm not trying to cause a fight, I'm just being realistic. I spent years deciphering how to safely navigate throughout Iyah, how to use the throne and the fairies' energy, and how to work the arch. It's a tricky place, at best."

Belle lifted her head, her voice bright. "The arch. He said the arch was gone."

"Who did?"

"The Jade King. He said that's why he couldn't go home. But *you* know how to open it," she said, her eyes lighting up. "You've talked about it before. If you can teach me, maybe I can open it and he will be forced home."

Shon thought about the notes hidden in the back of his pants. Those directions were in there, how to open the archway. And yet...if he gave them to her, the Jade King wouldn't return, he'd just resupply himself to stay longer in Iyah. Shon knew this. The Jade King wouldn't go willingly. He'd have to be forced through, and then the arch closed. But without the power of the throne...

"It's a moot point," Shon said. "Without control of the throne, you can't open it anyway. Only the Jade King can. At least, from Iyah." He paused. "Except...except the Jade King opened the archway from his own land. It took a lot of energy, but he did do it. If we could open it from *his* world, we could then push him through and he'd be stuck there."

Vic let out a snort. Shon and Belle glanced over at him.

"Excuse me, but we barely know how to get to Iyah. How the hell can we go to some new stone world and use a ton of energy to open some archway?"

Belle sighed. "He's got a point."

Shon lightly rapped his knuckles a few times on the tabletop. "I'm not sure. I'll have to think about it. But maybe there's a way."

"In the meantime," Belle said, "what should we do tonight? Do you think I'll end up by Bekk again or in the castle with the Jade King? What should we tell Bekk to do? And what do you think happened to Ashlee?"

"Hold on," Vic said. "We aren't *going* to Iyah. Not tonight, not ever."

Shon already forgot that just moments ago he'd been trying to convince them to leave Iyah well enough alone. But then he'd gotten wrapped up in the idea of saving the place again. What was wrong with him? How could he be willing to risk the lives of these teens, especially since he'd already lost his brother?

And yet, something inside him wouldn't release the idea. He felt bound to Iyah, he always had. His own bitterness and anger led him astray in that world and because of that, an obligation to make things right lingered deep inside. But what could he do? Traveling there himself was no longer an option. Perhaps he'd lost his opportunity to make amends. Perhaps it was time to let Iyah go.

Belle, apparently, didn't care how Shon *or* Vic felt.

"I'm not leavin' Ashlee there," she said, crossing her arms. "I can't and I won't."

"Even if that means you end up stuck there, too?" Vic asked.

"Yes!" she hissed.

A nurse glanced over and Shon gave a smile to indicate everything was all right. "Easy with the loud voices," he reminded the pair.

Vic huffed, crossing his arms.

Belle returned her gaze to Shon. "I want you to tell me anythin' else you remember, about Iyah, the throne, the doors to other worlds, the Jade King, everythin'."

"I'm gonna wait outside at the car," Vic said, standing abruptly.

Belle's face fell. "What? Vic, no, don't do that."

"I'm not okay with losing you, Belle," he said. "Bekk's dead. Ashlee is in a coma. And Shon, here, is in a mental institution. Nothing good comes from Iyah. Nothing." He turned and left.

Belle moved as if to go after him.

"Wait…" Shon said, reaching across the table and placing a hand on her arm. "Let him go. He just needs some time. I should know. I've tried giving up on Iyah several times."

"What made you go there again?"

"At first, a need to save my parents. But now? I'd give anything to return there, to help Bekk. But it's not Vic's fight. Or yours. Or even Ashlee's. It should be mine, but I'm not allowed to fight it anymore."

Belle spoke slowly at first. "I don't think it's all about you anymore, Shon. No offense. I mean, Ashlee is stuck there. It was her fairy that asked her to help Bekk. She's a part of this. And for some reason, Vic and I are a part of it, too. We were allowed to go there, even though we'd never gone as children. It wants us there, to help, to fight." Belle covered his hand with her own, her brown eyes sad, but determined. "I can't leave Ashlee there on her own. There must be somethin' you know that can help me."

"Well—"

"I can't *believe* this!" A high-pitched voice from behind him cut him off.

Shon whirled around. Standing a few feet away stood Treena. Shon immediately snatched his hand away from Belle's arm.

"It's not what you think," he said.

"Don't give me that," she snapped at him. "You two were holding hands. I *saw* it."

"No, it's n-not...it wasn't..." Belle stuttered.

"And *you*," Treena sneered. "I told you not to come back and visit Shon again, not after last time when you insinuated he'd want to be dead. How *dare* you come here again? But I guess I see why," she said with a sniff. She whipped her head again towards Shon.

"After all I've given up for you, this is the thanks I get? I don't know why I bothered with you. I'm outta here."

"Treena, wait!" Belle cried out, half-standing.

"Don't bother," Shon said, a sense of both relief and depression settling into his gut. "I think she's wanted a reason out from our relationship for a long time now. This just gives her an excuse and doesn't make her the 'bad guy.' She can save face and say I'm a cheater. Let her have this. Not like I'm going anywhere any time soon where I have to deal with the consequences." He sighed, remembering that soon enough he may be facing the outside world. Well, he could never be in her world again anyway. "This way she can move on from me, like she deserves."

Belle stayed quiet for a few more moments. "I'm sorry, Shon."

He shook his head. "It's okay. I can't give her a life."

"You aren't goin' to be in here forever, you know."

Looming thoughts of returning to life outside the hospital pressed down on him. "What do I have to look forward to out there?" The depression in his stomach spread into despair. "Listen," he said, reaching behind him. "I wrote everything down. About Iyah, all the stuff you just talked about it." He grabbed the two pages from his waistline, checked to make sure no one was watching, and then handed them to her. "If I've learned anything, it's that Iyah won't let you go, not if you're supposed to help. Which means, you've got to convince Vic to help again, too. You'll need him."

"What if he won't do it?"

"Iyah is...a strong place. Bekk got pulled there against his will and it almost drove him crazy. As for Ashlee, she may be okay, just stuck wherever she is. Why? I don't know. There's a piece to this puzzle that's missing for you."

"I'll do my best to find it," she said, tucking the pages into her purse.

Shon glanced at the clock. Visiting hours were almost over. "Listen," he said, "there's one more thing. If you return there, there's no guarantee you'll be with Bekk and Vic again. You may end up with the Jade King, if that's where Iyah *thinks* you're supposed to be."

"What does that mean?"

"Iyah brings people through their dreams and puts them wherever they need to be to work through their problems. That means if Iyah thinks you are supposed to be in the castle with the Jade King, it might put you there again."

"So I'm supposed to stop the king?"

"Maybe. But that doesn't mean you'll succeed. Iyah doesn't control you when you visit, only puts you where it wants you. I should know. I manipulated it for my own needs. It didn't stop me, it couldn't, but it did end up forcing my brother to come because he *could* stop me. Understand?"

Belle nodded. "I think so." She patted her purse, then paused. "I wish you could come with us."

Shon gave a weak smile. "There's a reason I'm not allowed in Iyah anymore. I messed everything up. Maybe you and Vic and Ashlee can make it right again." The despair had now spread through his body and for the first time in a week, he wanted to disappear into the bliss of his meds. Maybe he *wasn't* ready for the real world yet.

"If I do see Bekk, do you want me to tell him anythin'?"

Shon recalled how he'd heard his brother's voice a few days ago. An ache inside him grew stronger than even the despair.

"Tell him...tell him if he wants to let me know something, I'll hear him."

CHAPTER 10

Ashlee trotted behind the Jadari who, though about a foot shorter than her, moved rather quickly. The creatures scurried down the corridor and rounded a corner, which opened into a sweeping staircase going the opposite way from the front entrance. With her fingertips trailing lightly across the gemstone-embedded handrail, Ashlee tried to take in her surroundings while keeping an eye on where she stepped.

The rear entrance to the castle appeared just as dazzling as the front. With a graduating color scheme of red to gold along the walls, the ceiling congregated into a giant circle, with a rim of gold, a middle of what appeared to be pearl, and a center of stunning iridescent opal. Sparkling, glowing gemstones shone from the center, lighting up the vast room. Tall slitted windows lined the upper edges of the room and natural light struck the floor in slats, which fell directly between slabs of different colored gems to create light between each color of the rainbow.

Once at the bottom of the staircase, she was ushered through a set of glistening doors. A blue moon hung overhead, shining down on what she supposed were some sort of stables.

How long did we talk? she wondered.

Tall lampposts with orangey-red light lit up the area. The stables seemed to be set up like normal horse stables, except they glittered blue and purple in the dancing lava flames. She assumed sapphires comprised the bulk of the structure, with stalls for each animal and sacks of what appeared to be foodstuff next to them. Scents of ash and freshly wet cement filled the air.

The beasts inside each paddock shook their jeweled heads and made sounds at her approach. She pictured twinkling windchimes and searched for them for a moment before she realized the noise came from the beasts themselves. Ashlee's breath caught in her throat at the stunning creatures. They reminded her of the glass horse figurines her grandmother used to collect, except instead of completely clear, these beasts were each a different color, as if tinted by a different type of gemstone. Their bodies also were circular, like a blown glass doughnut sporting a horse's head.

They remind me of some of the Eclipse Sea creatures from home, Yir said, flittering around Ashlee's head.

The Gemstone woman had already settled onto one of the creatures, sitting in the center of the opening. She frowned. "You are too small to ride alone," she said to Ashlee. "I thought since you were bigger than the Jadari it may work, but I believe you will tumble off when mounted." She patted an area right in front of herself. "Please, join me."

Ashlee swallowed, both with fear and anticipation. She awkwardly climbed aboard, her hands slipping on the beast's smooth surface. It felt like trying to crawl up onto a glass mirror.

"The grooves," the Gemstone woman said, pointing out small indentations in the beast's hide.

"Thank you," Ashlee said, using the notches. Once she knew what to look for, she finished mounting. Slightly larger indentations were in front of her and she latched onto them with her hands. Yir took her newly chosen perch on Ashlee's shoulder, her tiny fingers and the tips of her batlike wings digging a bit into Ashlee's skin.

"The lysar is very fast, but I will keep you safe." The Gemstone woman wrapped a long, polished arm across Ashlee's shoulders and chest. Then, she emitted a strange trill, like the quick clinking of a fork against glass, and the beast took off.

Ashlee let out a shriek and gripped harder.

Wheeee! Yir cried out.

Once Ashlee understood the rhythm of the lysar, which moved by vibrating underneath her like a very powerful motorcycle, she relaxed into the movement. Suddenly, they'd reached the edge of the stables and raced through the doors held open by the Jadari.

Ashlee let out an audible gasp. The ground seemed to be littered with sapphires that glittered under the moonlight, just like the stable walls. She felt like she was zooming across a motionless sparkling sea. Ashlee tried not to think about how much worse it would be if she fell off onto such a hard surface. As they traveled, other gemstones slowly mixed with the sapphires—mostly emeralds and some sort of pale green stone she didn't know the name for.

Eventually, the sun began to rise and shone on all the gemstones surrounding them. She narrowed her eyes into slits to continue to see. In the distance, the largest mountains she'd ever seen in her life cut across the horizon. They looked like they were made of glass, but they glimmered and twinkled like diamonds.

"They can't be," she murmured. And yet, everything else here was made from gemstones. Why wouldn't their mountains be made of diamonds?

As they got closer, the lysar veered south, following the mountain line, but still several hundred meters away from their base. Ashlee could see why. A town came into view, with homes and buildings green and glowing, made of emeralds, lined with sapphires. Darkness, however, covered most of the area by what appeared to be storm clouds hanging over the village.

The lysar slowed and only then did Ashlee realize her face felt warm from the sun and her hair had been windswept all over. She quickly smoothed her blonde curls the best she could and waited until the lysar stopped before dismounting. Her leg muscles groaned with the effort. She hadn't realized they'd been gone so long, possibly riding for four hours, and the positioning of her body for that time left her achy.

Any thought of her own bodily pain was quickly pushed aside at the cries of people in the town.

"This is dangerous," the Gemstone woman told Ashlee, dismounting next to her with ease. "You should stay with the lysar." The beast made its twinkling noise again, having found a patch of...some sort of light blue stone, which it proceeded to grind in its mouth.

"All right," Ashlee said, eyeing the dark clouds overhead. The air felt dry and sooty, not like the humidity she usually experienced before a storm. She found a boulder of smooth emerald and took a seat. The Gemstone woman strode away towards the town, the satchel on her back bouncing with each step.

Several other gemstone people were moving in her direction, away from the village, their eyes wide with fear. Ashlee noted that they appeared to match their surroundings—their skin flush with blues and greens. She wondered why the Gemstone woman appeared so different, made up of multiple gems instead of just a few. A birth defect? A sign of Royal blood? Or perhaps they appeared this way based on where they lived or what they ate.

Before she could delve further into her thoughts, the Gemstone woman raised her arms.

"I have come," the Gemstone woman called out.

Many of the people stopped running. Some even cheered. The Gemstone woman disappeared into the throng of villagers and Ashlee lost sight of her.

Yir peeked her head out from Ashlee's hair. *What will the shiny lady do?*

"I don't know," Ashlee replied. "I guess stop the grim-shu, whatever that is."

Then, a noise filled the air that made Ashlee's skin prickle. A voice, like the slithering of an eel, crawled through the air.

"You are all so tasty!"

Though she knew it came from a distance, Ashlee still stood and moved closer to the lysar to gain some sense of protection. Yir returned to her hiding spot amongst Ashlee's locks of hair.

Villagers shrieked in the distance, though their cries seemed pale in comparison to the voice, which echoed out once again.

"I am *hungry!*"

Suddenly, Ashlee felt she'd made a mistake. She should have insisted she stay in the castle with the Jadari. Why had she thought coming here would be a good idea? Her mind must have been clouded with her experiences in Iyah, which had always been pleasant. But this was not Iyah. Who knew what would happen to her here?

"As soon as we get back," Ashlee whispered to Yir, "we are getting you to Iyah. This place isn't safe for us."

Yir responded with a scream inside Ashlee's head. Ashlee knew why. Something had flown up above the townspeople, hovering underneath the dark clouds and heading right at them. Its body was almost transparent, like a ghost from a movie, but there was a density to it, as if it had weight. Long arms stretched out in front of it, disproportional to its body, which seemed to be made of small boulders. It slid through the air and fell upon one of the fleeing townsfolk. The individual crumpled to the ground.

"Now!" the Gemstone woman yelled out from the distance.

Light shone everywhere. Ashlee shielded her eyes. The slithering voice hissed and shrieked. Peeking through the openings of her fingers, Ashlee watched as several villagers held up mirrored surfaces. The Gemstone woman stood directly across from Ashlee, holding up some sort of glowing stone, whose light ricocheted from all the mirrors, trapping the grim-shu in the middle.

With more hisses and cries like a wounded snake, the grim-shu contorted inside the light. Slowly, its limbs began to change, become more solid.

"Hold!" the Gemstone woman yelled.

The grim-shu gave one final hiss and then fell to the ground, fully tangible.

The glowing light ceased. The villagers put away their mirrored pieces and began to head towards to their town, slowly. Only the Gemstone woman approached the grim-shu body.

Ashlee, feeling that the danger had passed, trotted over to take a look. What she saw surprised her. A body, hardly taller than herself, though broader, lay there, made of dark gray stone. It looked almost nothing like the creature she just saw, except for traces of its body shape.

"That's a grim-shu?" Ashlee asked.

"No," the Gemstone woman said, her voice quiet. "That is a Basalt person."

"I don't understand."

By this time a few other townsfolk had returned with a make-shift stretcher. They placed the body on top of it and hauled it towards their village.

"Grim-shu are creatures of the mountains," the Gemstone woman said, her gaze following the fallen body. "They are both of this world and not of it. They did not appear until the Diamond Mountains rose. Since then, they sometimes enter our realm, when the sun and moon do not shine."

Ashlee eyed the storm clouds above them. Ash drifted down like large, soft snowflakes. "Like now."

"Precisely."

"But why did it turn into...a Basalt person?" Ashlee asked, remembering what the gemstone lady had called it.

"It began as a Basalt person who became infected by a grim-shu, then transformed into one. Once turned, hunger controls it. It will not rest until it feeds."

"But you all stopped it."

"Yes. Something I learned on my own. There were no records of grim-shu from my parents' time." The Gemstone woman paused a moment as the body moved out of sight, then began walking to the lysar. Ashlee jogged next to her.

"When the first grim-shu attacked, the creature consumed almost an entire village. I had been visiting there, speaking about a resin trade. The creature burst through the Diamond Mountains, raining down shards and pieces of diamond in its wake, as it had accidentally taken corporeal form before it cleared the mountain edge. One of the chunks of diamond fell in front of a lava lamp. The light of the lamp reflected off the diamond shard and the grim-shu fled from it. When I saw this, I took the piece and the lamp and followed it, forcing it to return to the mountain. But I could not kill it. Not until the next one arrived did I realize two things: the first, that the piece of diamond I'd found was somehow unique—only it would work and no other to reflect the light the way that was needed, and the second, that we required a way to trap the grim-shu inside the light. That is what you saw, with the reflectors the villagers carried."

The two of them remounted the lysar and Ashlee let out a low whistle. "So that's why you have to come here, because you are the only one with the diamond chunk that works."

"Yes. The lysar let me move quickly to a territory that may need the diamond. It has proven to be the fastest way to get the diamond to the place needing to demolish a grim-shu."

"And the Basalt person? They didn't survive?"

"They never do."

A few moments of silence passed as the lysar began its return journey to the castle. "Is there a way to purge the grim-shu from the mountains?"

"Unfortunately not. The mountains are impenetrable. Even worse, they are spreading."

Ashlee's forehead furrowed. "The grim-shu?"

"The mountains."

"How can mountains spread?"

"They were formed by unnatural ways. They continue to grow, to encroach inland. We can barely keep them at bay as is."

"But if they are impenetrable, how can you stop them?"

Ashlee heard the Gemstone woman yawn. "When the first grim-shu broke through, the crack it came from sealed itself up, but we discovered that the diamond pieces created by the breakage could cut through other diamonds. We've been using those pieces to keep the expanding mountains at bay. It is a constant struggle and many of my people spend their lives simply doing that one activity. Unfortunately, the pieces are wearing down and the supply lessens as time passes. Eventually, we will not be able to hold the mountains at bay, and my dominion will become nothing but solid diamond."

Ashlee remained quiet for the rest of the journey, overcome by the image of diamond slowly rolling across the land, covering and killing anything in its way, like a glacier in an ice age. When they arrived at the castle and dismounted, Ashlee finally spoke again.

"Is there any way to stop the diamonds from taking over?"

The Gemstone woman blinked several times, fatigue on her face. "That is why I have been trying to use my creatures in the arch to capture someone who works for the Jade King. I am hoping that a truce between our people will dissolve the mountains and save my dominion from extinction. But truthfully? I do not know if anyone from the Jade Kingdom would even care to help us at this point."

CHAPTER 11

Dark green jade walls encircled Jayman. He'd been in the Jade Castle's dungeon for about two days with no idea as to when he might be released. He hadn't seen anyone but the guards who'd hauled him from his inn the moment he'd arrived there. They'd questioned him first about the whereabouts of the princess, Jayla. When he told them he didn't know where she'd gone, they'd ransacked his place and cleared out his customers. Afterwards, they arrested him and took him to the castle. He'd been here ever since.

There wasn't anything particularly *wrong* with being in the dungeon. It wasn't cold or dry. A bed had been provided as well as a lava lamp. He'd been fed regularly. The main difficulty was that no one would speak to him. When he first arrived, they told him he would be brought before the Jade King, but this "meeting" hadn't occurred and the guards refused to say anything more about when it might take place.

Jayman found the entire situation odd. He'd just met the Jade King a few days before. Though definitely the largest man he'd ever seen, he'd gotten the impression the Jade King would want to talk with him as soon as possible if it had to do with one of his children. So where was he?

During his incarceration, Jayman's thoughts flittered between his Beloved and his inn, hoping both fared well during his absence. He also wondered about Jayla and hoped *she'd* made it to a safe destination also. Jayman had grown quite fond of Jayla—she reminded him of a niece he hadn't seen in ages—and after what she'd just gone through, he cared about her wellbeing. To learn in such a short period of time that her brother had been killed by her own father, that a Jadari predicted it, and that she had gifts as an... oracle...

Oracle.

Jayman shook his head at the word. The changes must have been overwhelming to the young woman. If you'd asked him even a week ago what he thought about someone who could see into the future or into other people's lives, he would have laughed it off. But after witnessing Jayla's storytelling at his own inn? After seeing the enraptured faces of his patrons while she spoke? And feeling that same amazement inside himself, as though she told the story only for him, and it was the most important thing he'd ever hear in his life.

He'd been convinced, although, as a lowly innkeeper, he didn't think he could do anything with that information except hope Jayla had survived.

A strange scraping noise sounded down the hall. Then a muffled thump. Finally, a clatter.

Jayman pressed against the stone bars, straining to see what had happened.

A face appeared in his view and he bit back a shriek. It was not a guard.

"We must hurry," the person said, holding a tool to loosen the bolt on the cell so the door would open.

Jayman finally placed the figure. "Taker Jayro?"

"Yes, Innkeeper," Taker Jayro said. His low voice resonated inside the corridor.

In awe, Jayman asked, "What are you doing here?"

"Much has happened in the past week," he said, unbolting the final lock. He slid the door open and gestured for Jayman to follow. "First, we must hurry. We do not have a lot of time. And stay quiet."

Jayman immediately tensed and kept close to the bulky man. He'd met Taker Jayro about a week ago, when the man came to the inn to listen to Jayla's story. In charge of the M.A.G.M.A. Institute—which catered to the mentally and emotionally ill—he'd come in order to purchase Jayla's tale, if he thought it meaningful enough to do so. Full of doubt and snide remarks, Taker Jayro did not believe someone of Jayla's age could have a reasonable story to tell, but was also curious because of what he'd heard from others. He, like Jayman, did not realize Jayla didn't tell her own stories, but those of others.

However, once Taker Jayro heard Jayla speak, he'd fallen to his knees, and confessed that he knew Jayla to be an oracle. A patient of his, a Basalt woman, told him that a Jade woman would tell a specific tale. That same story was the one Jayla told in Jayman's inn.

But that did not explain Taker Jayro's presence now. He could not have known about Jayman's arrest by the castle guards. So how could he be here?

Jayman's question halted in his mind when he noticed an unconscious guard at the end of the corridor. Tiptoeing, he held his breath while they passed, watching closely to spot any signs of movement.

Once out of earshot, he whispered, "How are we going to get out of here?" A single guard was one thing, but how had Taker Jayro managed to enter the castle against all the other soldiers? Had he brought an army? A mob?

Taker Jayro put a finger to his lips, signifying for Jayman to stay quiet. He then moved against the wall, eyes closed.

Jayman just stood there.

Taker Jayro opened his eyes. They narrowed. With a forceful gesture, he indicated that Jayman should also stand flat against the wall.

Jayman followed suit, unsure of what—

A sucking sensation rushed through Jayman, starting where his stone skin contacted the wall and moving through his body outwards. When Jayman made a move to pull away from the wall, Taker Jayro's arm shot out and crossed his chest, holding him in place. Before he could resist, the pulling took over, and Jayman was absorbed into the wall.

For several moments he couldn't breathe. He couldn't see. Only a sense of liquidity stole through him. Then, almost as soon as the sensation had begun, his vision returned, showing him a new room. Air entered his lungs. And finally he could move his arms and legs.

Taker Jayro stood next to him, taking in deep breaths.

"Traveling that way is still unsettling," Taker Jayro said, "even to me. I'm sorry I could not warn you."

"What *was* that?" Jayman gasped.

"The Jadari's mode of transportation," Taker Jayro replied, shaking his limbs.

A sickly sort of gooey feeling still resided in his own arms, so Jayman rubbed them while he pondered the Jadari. Before a few days ago, Jayman hadn't given the subservient creatures a second thought. From what he knew, they existed in the Jade Castle solely to serve the Royal Family. They somehow survived by being part of the structure of the walls. And they didn't speak.

Yet five days ago he'd heard one speak to warn Jayla of the demise of her brother and to flee the castle grounds.

To be here, now, and having moved through the walls like the Jadari? Jayman's head spun. He was not equipped to deal with any of this. As a simple man with a simple life, he'd only wanted to see the castle, not get wrapped up in a Royal mess.

Regardless of what you want, you are out of that cell, he told himself. *Make the best of it.* Those five words had gotten him through hard times in the past. He hoped they would help him now as well.

Getting his bearings, Jayman took in his new surroundings. They stood in a bedroom, more lavish than Jayman had ever seen, with rusty-red jasper lights embedded into the walls and a jasper chandelier hanging from the ceiling, a portrait of the Royal Family hanging on one of the walls, a generously-sized bed, and a huge, gaping archway across from him.

Jayman stared at the blackness in the wall. He shivered. The space felt...wrong. The darkness didn't seem natural, and yet he didn't know how to explain it otherwise. It just should not exist, not in this room, not in this world.

He quickly averted his gaze to Taker Jayro. "Thank you," he said, "for helping me to escape. But I'm not sure how, or what's going on? How did you even know I was being held there? And..." he said, looking around the room, "...where are we exactly?"

"We are in the Jade King's personal quarters."

Jayman's body went cold. "You must be joking." His line of sight skipped over to the closed door, expecting at any moment for a guard or the king himself to crash through.

"Do not worry," Taker Jayro said. "We are secure for right now. The Jadari know the castle. They have led us here because it is safe."

"Safe? How?"

"The Jade King is gone."

A pause. "What do you mean 'gone?' As in crumbled?"

"No. Missing from the Jade Kingdom." Taker Jayro took a few steps towards the archway. Jayman almost reached out to stop him from getting too close. He knew, somehow, that nothing good could come from that arch.

Without warning, Jayman's body began to shake. It was as if all the events from the past week finally caught up with him. He took a seat on the edge of the bed, deciding to ask questions to keep himself distracted until he calmed down.

"Taker Jayro, I must know, what has happened since I last saw you? Obviously, you've been in contact with the Jadari, but how? And how did they know to bring you to me?"

Taker Jayro, keeping a bit of distance between him and the arch, cocked his head as if studying it. His eyes traced the symbols around the edges of the archway while he spoke.

"After I left your inn, I returned to the M.A.G.M.A. Institute in search of the Basalt woman who had told me of Jayla's story."

Jayman nodded. "I remember. You said she predicted the tale Jayla would tell."

"Indeed. When I arrived, she was taking her final breaths. She'd apparently waited long enough for me to return, to do one last thing."

"Which was?"

Taker Jayro turned for a moment and peered at Jayman. "To instruct me to find the Jadari at the quarries of Jayadin City and to save you."

A shudder ran through Jayman that had nothing to do with his physical condition. "She knew about me? And about my predicament?"

Taker Jayro's gaze returned to the wall. "Yes. But I did not know what she meant. You seemed fine when I'd left you earlier that day. Since the oracle had been right about Jayla, I realized I didn't have to understand, I only needed to heed her words. So the next morning I set out to the jade quarry deposits that lined the northwestern edge of the city. As far as I knew, Jadari only lived in the castle."

Jayman nodded with agreement.

"Apparently, we've all been mistaken." Taker Jayro brushed his fingertips against the wall near the arch's edge and Jayman flinched.

"Go on," Jayman urged, fearing that somehow at any moment Taker Jayro would be drawn into that inky void.

"I didn't know what to do. I searched the area for hours with no results. Finally, I gave up and returned to the institute. But the urge to follow the Basalt woman's words gnawed at me throughout the night. I had dreams of moving walls of jade and losing my balance, forcing me to rest against them. When I woke, I returned to the quarry, took a deep breath, and stood flat against the side of a wall."

"You were sucked in?" Jayman guessed.

"Correct. Just like what happened to us in the dungeon. I emerged near the castle stables, surrounded by Jadari. They implored me to keep quiet and to watch the courtyard. There, I saw you, and the princess."

Jayman remembered all too well. He and Jayla had been admiring the night-blooming quartz and staring up into the sky. Then...

"The Jadari's warning," Jayman muttered.

"Precisely. The shock of hearing one of them speak..." Taker Jayro paused in his movements.

"I know the feeling."

Taker Jayro resumed his search, though for what, Jayman couldn't tell. "I watched as the princess fled, how you remained in the courtyard, waiting for her return. I wanted to say something, let you know I was there, but the Jadari stopped me. They indicated I must stay quiet, so I did. With easy-to-interpret gestures, they signaled that I needed to help the two of you escape the grounds. They pointed towards the nearest exit doors, where two guards stood at attention."

Realization hit Jayman. "The doors were unguarded and open when Jayla returned, allowing us to leave uncontested. That was *you?*"

Taker Jayro stopped his search and faced Jayman. "The guards were not permanently damaged, but yes, I got them out of the way and opened the doors for you. Then I hid outside. I didn't even know if you'd gotten out because as soon as I leaned against the castle wall, I was absorbed once again and redeposited at the quarry. The Jadari told me I must return in four days. I didn't know why, but I told them I would.

"Later that day, after I returned to work," he continued, "I saw the announcement with the princess's picture on it, requesting information about her whereabouts. I knew the two of you had escaped."

"It seems you waited until today and the Jadari led you to me. But how do you know about the Jade King's absence?"

"The Basalt woman's final story."

Jayman's face creased in confusion.

"Storytelling is a way for my patients to mend," he said, "which is why new stories are always so valuable. I have my patients retell parts of their lives, to help them stay grounded and connected to our stone earth. But the Basalt woman never wrote down any story except the one about Jayla. That's why I remembered it. However, the night before she crumbled, she wrote something down in secret. No one told me about it because the pages weren't found until they cleaned out her quarters. She'd hidden the sheets of stone under her bed."

"What did the story say?"

"It spoke of a king, a king who'd gotten lost. He traveled through the blackness of an archway in his room and emerged victorious, only to be thwarted by his own impatience. It said he would not return home, not unless…"

"Unless what?"

"The tale ended there."

A sinking feeling trickled down through Jayman's body. He thought for sure the oracle's words would help them. "Then this is the arch?" His eyes now met the entranceway with more reverie.

"Yes."

"What are you looking for?"

A look of anger stole across Taker Jayro's face. "A way to close it. Forever."

CHAPTER 12

"You again!" the Jade King snarled. He glared down at the young pinkish woman in front of him. She'd simply appeared, as if she'd been there all along, but invisible. Some time had passed after she'd vanished and when he couldn't find her in the bedroom, he'd returned to the throne room.

She let out a sigh. "*You* again," she repeated, crossing her arms. She tilted her head. "I see your gracious attitude at me being your 'guest' has already come and gone."

The Jade King's jaw ground back and forth. "You left when you claimed you would stay. For all I knew, to plot my demise. You were very vocal about the monster you believe I am."

The young woman's eyes softened and she lowered her arms. "You're right. My Mama always told me not to judge someone based on what others said, but by how they treated me. I'm sorry."

The Jade King stood still, skeptical. "An apology?" He wondered if this was some sort of trick. She could obviously come and go as she pleased. He could not trust her.

"I'm not sayin' we'll be friends, I'm just sayin' I'm sorry I was quick to judge." She scrunched up her nose, as if thinking. "My name's Belle," she told him.

The Jade King searched her face for deception. Regardless of his fears, a part of him found comfort in her return. He had enjoyed the company.

"I am the Jade King," he replied.

Her gaze flickered up to the crown on his head. "That makes sense."

"How are you in this world?" he asked, taking a seat on the throne. He found he didn't like being away from it for too long. It gave him comfort, a sense of safety. "You mentioned before you are not of this world. If not, then why have you come here, to the castle, instead of staying with your friends?"

"Why should I answer that?" she retorted.

"I told you of the reason for *my* being here. It makes sense for you to reciprocate."

Belle's lips smacked. "Seems fair. The answer is...I didn't choose to come to the castle. And I don't know how long I'll stay."

"So you plan to leave again?" Curiosity crept up his spine. If she could move through to another world, perhaps there was a way that he could as well.

"It's...not in my control. I don't know what brings me here."

Disappointment replaced curiosity. The Jade King drummed his fingertips on the chair's arm.

"Then why would a force bring you here?"

A long breath was expelled though her nose. "That is a good question."

"You do not know?"

"I'm...I thought I knew, when I first got here. But everythin' became...complicated."

He felt the same way. "What was your original purpose here?"

"To help my friend." She held up a hand. "I'm not goin' to tell you about him so don't even ask."

The Jade King nodded, understanding her reluctance. "Since these complications arose, do you have a new purpose here?"

"I'm not sure. To be honest," she said, her large eyes staring at him, "I think I'm here to help you."

That got the Jade King's attention. "Help *me*? How?"

"I don't know."

"You seem to have a large lack of knowledge."

She rolled her eyes. "Yeah, I got that. But at least I'm not stuck here."

The Jade King frowned, but inwardly smiled at her banter. "Then what do you propose?"

Belle sighed. "I sound like a broken record, but I really don't know."

Though unfamiliar with her vocabulary as to what a "record" was, he understood her point. At that moment, several of his guards returned.

"Anything?" the Jade King asked, eagerness in his voice.

Silence.

He took that as a "no."

An eerie sense of something wrong passed over him. He stared at his guards. Their numbers seemed...less. Far less. He'd brought

300 with him. He knew some had remained in the castle, guarding the entrances and exits, but only about two dozen stood before him.

"Where are the rest of the guards?" He knew he'd instructed them to spread out, find a fairy, and bring it to the castle, but to only walk a day's worth of time and then return.

Silence.

"What's wrong with them?" Belle asked.

The Jade King jumped. He'd forgotten about the girl. "They are..." He wasn't sure what to say. He didn't like the idea of telling Belle that he had control over the guards' free will, that they could move and do things he asked, but they couldn't verbally respond or think for themselves.

Why do I care what she thinks? he wondered. He'd dealt with dozens of delegates from all over the land and never felt he had to care about their opinions of him. *It must be this place,* he thought. *It softens me. Without a connection to my world, I will become weaker. I must find a way home!*

"They are my Royal Guards," he said. "They don't speak." The lie felt odd on his tongue, but he forced the feeling away.

"That must suck," Belle said, gazing at the soldiers.

"I do not understand."

"Oh, sorry. I mean, that's lousy, like it's not great. That must be hard, to not have anyone to talk to." She grinned. "Good thing I'm here. I usually can't seem to keep quiet."

The Jade King felt the inkling of that same inward smile form on his lips. This girl, if nothing else, was amusing.

Suddenly, one of the guards moaned, as if in terrible pain. The

Jade King stood up from the throne. Belle gasped.

The soldier's eyes lost their pearly look and life returned to them. "Help me," she cried out. Then, in the most surreal sense, the Jade King watched her...melt. He couldn't think of a better word for it. The guard's body turned to liquid, like the consistency of the pearly substance he'd used to control her, and became a puddle on the floor.

"What the hell just happened?" Belle cried out, pointing at the gooey mess.

The Jade King had absolutely no idea. It was as if he'd lost his control, but instead of the soldier merely regaining her will, she'd died. Why had this happened? "I do not know."

"So that's not normal?"

"Not at all." He wandered over to the green shiny puddle and stared down at it. His reflection stared back.

Again, without any warning, another guard went through the same process. Then a third. A fourth. All twenty-something guards melted before his eyes. He heard Belle shrieking behind him as he moved away, just as horrified. What was happening to them?

"I gotta get out of here," Belle said, edging towards the door.

"My guards outside will not let you leave," he told her.

"Are they even there anymore?"

The Jade King didn't have an answer.

"Somethin' is wrong," she said, shaking her head. "Somethin' has gone terribly wrong!" She fled.

"Wait!" he cried out, but she had already moved out of the area. The Jade King viewed the scene in horror. He strode towards the doorway of the throne room and peered outside. The girl had disappeared. Two puddles lay on either side of the door. His guards were all gone.

Aloneness coated him like a layer of crushed ash.

The Jade King returned to the throne, seeking comfort in its contours, solace in its authority. He could feel its strength flowing through him.

With eyes that stared across the room at nothing, he gripped the arms of the chair.

A mantra of reassurance filtered through his mind.

He still had the throne. He still had the power.

CHAPTER 13

Only about an hour had passed since Vic disappeared to his own reality and Bekk hadn't done much more than walk through the Sunbeam Forest before his friend popped up right in front of him.

"Holy crap, man!" Bekk exclaimed. "You came out of nowhere." He took a beat. "Wait, why are you here so soon?"

"What do you mean?" Vic asked. "It's been a whole day since I saw you."

Bekk remembered. "The time difference. That's right. I can never predict how long time passes here versus on Earth." He paused again. "I thought you weren't going to come back here if you didn't have to?"

"I wasn't. I mean, I didn't want to. But Belle...well...she can be pretty persuasive."

Bekk smiled at the reference to his friend. He'd known Belle for over five years. "I hear you. Regardless, I'm glad you did." A quick glance showed Belle wasn't nearby. "Speaking of, where is she?"

"Most likely with the Jade King again," Vic said, a touch of anger in his voice.

"What do you mean? What's going on?"

Vic rubbed his hand against a nearby tree. "Long story short? We, me and Belle I mean, went to see your brother again."

Bekk's voice caught in his throat. "Just the *two* of you?"

"Yeah. Ashlee still hasn't woken up."

Bekk forced himself to stay calm. At least she hadn't died, which meant she existed somewhere, just unable to return to her body. That indicated she could still be okay. "So what did Shon have to say?"

"A lot. He even wrote a bunch of information down for us cuz he doesn't get a lot of time in the hospital to chitchat."

"Well seeing as how we never know how long you'll stay either, maybe you should give me the CliffsNotes version."

"All right. Basically, we learned three main things. One, Iyah puts us wherever it wants, so even if we don't want to come here, it may not matter."

Again, Bekk noticed a tinge of irritation to his words.

"Second, we learned about the archway, and how to create it while using the throne. But it doesn't sound like something we can do."

Bekk perked up at this comment, since he hadn't been able to open the arch up, even though he'd copied what his brother had done. Maybe Vic couldn't do it, but Bekk wanted to try.

"And third, since Ashlee is in a coma, Shon thinks she's just stuck here somewhere, but that she's not dead."

"That's what I just thought, too." Bekk took a few moments to assess his friend. Vic seemed tired, frustrated, and resigned. "You didn't have to come," Bekk said.

"Doesn't sound like I would have had much of a choice. You didn't. Figured at least this way it's my decision instead of getting yanked here against my will."

Bekk didn't know what to say. He'd always loved this place when he'd been younger—it had literally been a way for him to escape his tough life. But now? It had its own power. It was messing up his friends' lives. And his girlfriend was in a coma, stuck somewhere with no way to find her.

"This place stinks," Bekk said, kicking aimlessly at the dirt.

Vic turned to look at Bekk. "I knew you were frustrated, but I thought you liked it here?"

"You think I wanted to stay?" Bekk threw up his arms in frustration. "It seemed so noble at the time, saving these fairies, stopping my brother. But now? This place is messing with so many people. And I'm here all by myself and some king is taking over and the fairies don't even seem to care!"

Vic glanced around. "Yeah...where are they?"

"Dealing with kids."

"Kids?"

"Yeah. That's their job. They help troubled children in their dreams. Helps them escape, have a friend, and reestablish their confidence, so they can find real friends and make it through their hardships in the real world."

"Sounds like something Cal could use..." Vic muttered.

It took a minute for Bekk to place the name. "Your younger brother?"

"Yeah."

"Is he still having trouble? I remember you said he was acting out."

"Yeah. The fights at school are getting worse. He got into a yelling match with my dad a few months ago. Then, for a little bit, he seemed okay again. But these past few weeks? He's seriously out of control."

Slivers of memory wafted through Bekk's mind. "You said... you said he 'missed his dreams.'"

A touch of a frown lingered on Vic's mouth. "Yeah. Yeah, that sounds like something he said. I mean, it was a while ago." His forehead wrinkled. "Come to think of it, he mentioned something about it last week when he was yelling at my dad. Something about...how my dad didn't understand. How he wished..." Vic's dark skin paled to an almost ashy brown. "Oh God, Bekk, he said how he wished he could stay asleep, but even his dreams didn't help anymore."

Tension crept up around them. "Do you think...?" Bekk asked.

"That Cal comes to Iyah in his sleep?" He nodded vigorously.

Somehow Bekk had forgotten that he hadn't just stayed here to save the fairies. He stayed because of what they did for others. And not just on Earth. They catered to problematic children and creatures in different worlds. What they did here was important.

Iyah may bring them here, may screw up their lives, but it was so much bigger than just them.

Determination filled Bekk. "I know you may not want to be here. And for a long time now, even though I didn't want to admit it, I didn't want to be here anymore either. But I forgot. I forgot why I did what I did to stop my brother. And now this king, or whatever, is messing with the very thing I died for. And all those kids...they deserve a place they can go and be safe."

Color returned to Vic's face. "I didn't think about that."

Bekk playfully punched him in the shoulder. "Why would you, man?"

Vic smiled briefly. "Well, now what?"

"The good news is, we have some time. You and Belle seem to be able to safely return home and if things get too crazy, you don't have to come here."

"But Shon said Iyah can make you return."

"Maybe. But not right away. And not easily. I battled with coming here for months before Ryf had enough power to bring me here. If things get too bad, I know you two can figure out how to stay away for a while."

"Maybe." Vic scoffed before his face became somber. "Like you said, it's not really about us anymore. I mean, if I can help fix this place for Cal, I will."

"Okay. Let's go into a little more detail about what my brother told you. Maybe we can find a weakness in the Jade King, or at least his plan."

"Right. Okay, well—"

Vic was interrupted by a group of four fairies who flew out of the forest from the south. Their voices overlapped each other in

Bekk's mind and he held up his hands.

"Hold on!" he cried out. "One at a time!" A turquoise fairy began to speak, his voice soft but urgent.

Bekk, the fairies have been looking everywhere for you.

"What's the matter?" Vic asked Bekk.

Bekk shushed him and continued to listen.

We just came from the Sugar Caves. Each of us were supposed to meet with a child. But no one showed up.

"The kids they were supposed to help didn't show up," Bekk relayed to Vic. "Why not?" he asked the fairy.

We aren't sure. This has never happened before.

A pink fairy spoke up, his voice deep and reverberating inside Bekk's skull.

Tell him about the mist.

I'm getting to that! the turquoise fairy snapped, its soft tone disappearing in an instant. *At the very southern edge of the Sugar Caves, I noticed a mist. It had never been there before. I went to look at it and could see other creatures inside it.*

"Something dangerous?" Bekk asked.

No. Other Iyah creatures. To help children from other worlds. But their domain does not extend to the Sugar Caves. And one of the creatures looked at me—they were as confused as I was. But even worse, the mist began coming closer, crossing the boundary line of the caves!

"Okay, let me think." He took a few moments to tell Vic what had just transpired.

"What does that mean?" Vic asked. "That an entire area is

moving?"

"It sounds like it. But why? Is it shifting? Is the Jade King moving it somehow?"

Suddenly, five more fairies approached from deep in the forest, this time from the east.

"What's going on?" Bekk asked them.

They relayed the same story about the lack of children and a moving colored area, except the boundary crossing took place straight east, at the edge of the Sunbeam Forest.

"Mist?" Bekk asked.

No, a yellow fairy said. *Like an orange wall. It almost looked like fire, but there was no heat. Not until I touched it with my finger and it burned!*

"And it was moving towards you, into the forest?"

Yes, but the trees did not burn. They just were covered with the orange wall.

Bekk repeated the information to Vic. "It's like Iyah is shifting or moving," Bekk concluded.

"Or collapsing," Vic suggested.

The idea percolated in Bekk's mind. "Oh my God, you're right. I think Iyah *is* collapsing. And..." he said, taking in the fairies' directional information, "it seems like it's pushing north and west." Bekk peered around. "That means...we have to move north, up the coastline again."

"Guess we *don't* have as much time as we thought," Vic said. "But if we go north again, won't those soldiers just grab us?"

"We'll have to take our chances and stick close to the

shoreline." Bekk then addressed the fairies. "Go find any other fairies you can. We need to regroup. Also, find out where else this is happening. We will meet up where this firestream meets the sea."

The fairies all raced off in different directions.

The two young men began to trot west.

"Why is this happening?" Vic asked.

"I don't know. Maybe it has to do with the Jade King. Maybe he's throwing everything off balance."

"How could he do that? And won't the collapsing areas hurt him?"

"No clue. Maybe this was his plan all along: to destroy Iyah. Or he may have figured out a way to stay protected in the castle, to force us to move towards him."

"Those options aren't promising."

Bekk didn't answer, focusing instead on keeping his breathing steady while they jogged. About a half hour later, they reached the churning of the firestream rushing into the water. They both caught their breath as they waited for the fairies to return.

"Okay," Bekk said, facing Vic. "Now, tell me everything my brother said to you when you spoke to him last." Before Vic began, Bekk had a stray thought, so strong it was almost as if he'd spoken out loud. *I wish you were here, Shon.*

CHAPTER 14

"I wish you were here, Shon."

Shon bolted into an upright position. He'd been asleep, but struggling to wake up. Dreams invaded his mind, disturbing dreams of the archway, of small black creatures trying to drag him into its darkness, into oblivion. And yet, he couldn't fully awaken. Not until he heard his brother's voice.

Sweat glistened on his arms and chest as moonlight poured through the window of his room in the institution. His roommate snored on, as no amount of noise from Shon's side ever stopped that young man from sawing logs.

Chilled to the bone, Shon rubbed his limbs and pulled the covers up to his chin. Eventually the shaking stopped, but a myriad of thoughts and feelings raced through him. Why was he dreaming about the archway? He hadn't had any dream related to Iyah since he'd been banished. Was it a message? Was he about to die? Did the black creatures want his soul for all the wrong he'd done?

Another shudder ripped through him. He didn't want to die, but the arch responded to that desire. Had someone on the other side figured out a way to use the arch to kill people against their will?

Too many questions that he didn't have the answers to.

One thing, though, was clear. His brother needed him. But what could Shon do? He was stuck, unable to help, unable to reach Iyah.

Sleep wouldn't return. All he could do for now was wait and call Belle or Vic tomorrow to see what was going on in Iyah.

CHAPTER 15

The mokaki, a smaller yet broader breed related to the moki mounts Jayla was used to, squirmed underneath her. Though the movement came naturally to the beast, Jayla found it unsettling, as though it wanted to both dive down and fly up at the same time. She couldn't quite get the rhythm and after the first half hour of riding, she gave up, and dozed fitfully until the sun rose in the sky.

The land stretched in greys and ash tones, the surface craggy and rocky. The mokaki were built for this type of terrain and Jayla knew if she had her moki here, it would have been slipping and sliding on the uneven surface. A large crater lay to the west—a quarry for basalt mining. As they rode further southwest, several natural basalt caverns and cliffsides surrounded them, with striated rockfaces, like long strips of rock vertically laid next to each other. At first, she thought the neutrality of the color might get boring, but the slight variations and the hypnotic lines captivated her.

Then, when rounding a final corner, the rockiness flattened out, revealing the small town of Bagen in the distance.

Jayla gasped at the sight. Looming behind the village stood the

Diamond Mountains—huge and glorious and shining in the morning's light. They sparkled more than any polished stone Jayla had ever seen. And they rose, and rose, into the pale ash clouds above until they disappeared.

"Three 'ours or so left," Basala called out behind him, one of the few times he'd bothered to speak to her at all. He urged his mount forward and Jayla did her best to keep up.

Three hours until they reached Bagem Market, to procure the gems she needed as an elixir to return her after becoming a grimshu. At first, Jayla hadn't been that worried. The voice in her head, though unsettling, only came once in a while, speaking of eating tasty things. She'd been able to tune it out.

But as they approached the marketplace around midday, with its scents and smells, Jayla realized she was not enticed by what she first thought—vats of simmering soups and chunks of smoked stone—but the people themselves who smelled delicious to her.

Without warning, the voice came in, loud and clear. *If I can have just one...*

Jayla shivered, even though the sun shone bright and warm. This was the first time the voice spoke as if she herself were speaking. An ache in her stomach jabbed at her insides. She'd never felt so hungry in her life.

"Basala," she moaned. Her body tipped to the side and she fell off her mount.

In a flash, her guide spun his beast, grabbed her mokaki by the reigns, and came to her aide. "Are you 'urt?" he asked.

"Hungry," she muttered.

Just one bite...

"Look at me," he said, forcing her face upwards. He studied her, his black eyes darting back and forth. "Too fast," he murmured. "We must 'urry." He grabbed her by the arms and yanked her upwards, draping her over his shoulder as if she weighed no more than a thin slab of limestone. He then began to trot, the reigns of both mokaki in his free hand, and headed towards the nearest stables, which sat on the edge of the market.

"Oi!" he called out. A short, pale gray Basalt child scurried over. His eyes widened at the sight of Jayla slung over Basala's shoulder. "Feed 'em and water 'em. I'll come get 'em in an 'our."

"Yessir." The young child grabbed the reins, did a quick glance once again at Jayla, then led the mokaki to the stables.

Basala hiked straight through the marketplace, ignoring the luring calls of merchants, to a tent towards the back.

"Put me down!" Jayla cried out, struggling. The gawking stares of those around her made her feel extremely uncomfortable. They all stopped selling their wares, safe behind stony stands with different colored banners. Smells of food repulsed her. She wanted them and their living, rocky flesh.

"'Ush," he ordered. When they reached the tent, he plunked her down and shoved her through the open flap.

"How *dare* you!" she demanded. "How dare you treat me that way, like a common sack of quartz chips."

"Look," Basala said, pointing at her arms.

Jayla glanced down and all the fire inside her went out.

She could see through her arms.

He wants to stop you, to stop us, to stop me, the voice said. *Don't let him. Get him. Eat him. Stop* him.

Jayla lurched to the side, grabbing hold of the tent pole nearby. "I don't want this," she said. Fear crawled around in her gut, competing with the pangs of hunger. "I want to stay me. I don't want to change."

Meanwhile, the occupants of the tent scurried around, chatting with Basala, grabbing crystals from behind the counter. They stared at her, their eyes full of their own fear and a touch of hatred. She could tell. She could taste it in the air. They felt it had been her fault for getting infected in the first place.

It's not my fault, the voice said. *I didn't ask for this. I just want to be left alone, to be free inside the mountain. They make me want to eat them. They are so tasty.*

The leader of the tent, a bulky Basalt woman with untrusting eyes, shouted orders. Three of the other Basalt people in the area attempted to corral Jayla towards the far side of the tent. The woman held three crystals in her hand and placed them on the counter to grind.

No! Without thinking, Jayla ducked under the outstretched arms of one person and lashed out at the counter. She struck at the crystals, sending them flying.

"It's too fast," the leader of the tent said. "Get it contained!"

Why are they calling me an "it?" Jayla wondered, though her thought sounded far away.

They fear me. They do not understand. I must be free. I must be free!

Jayla could hear multiple voices in the tent, calling out different things. They all sounded like a strange din and she couldn't differentiate what they were saying.

She wanted to run. The Diamond Mountains called to her. They beckoned her, with their coldness and their isolation. She could roam without any responsibilities. Being an oracle would mean nothing. Stopping her father held no value. Caring about her deceased brother could end.

The sound of grinding in the background cut through the white noise. Her eyes narrowed in on the woman who currently broke down the crystals that would revert her.

Stop her!

Jayla lunged again, but this time something hard struck her across the shoulders, knocking her down.

A growl emerged from her lips.

"Look! It's almost changed!"

Jayla shook her head, registering the words. She peered at herself. Her limbs were almost completely transparent.

"It'll become untouchable. 'Urry!" Basala shouted at the woman behind the counter. Jayla could see her pour some sort of thick paste over the ground crystals. "We gotta get this in 'er before it turns completely!"

Jayla lunged again, this time at Basala.

Yes. Strip him of his stony skin!

He caught her in the face this time with another blow. She rolled backwards, growling once more. Basala swiped at her again and she dodged, moving sideways, closer to the woman. As a slithering wisp, she moved *through* two of the others and reached the counter, becoming tangible once more.

"NOW!"

Hands grabbed her. She shrieked, squirming. Someone pried open her mouth. Hot liquid, like molten lava, ran down her throat. She coughed and wretched, but to no avail. The fluid entered her. She could feel it, like a burning stone in the pit of her stomach.

"No!" she screeched. She flung her arm behind her, momentarily turning intangible, then solidifying at the right moment. She struck one of them in the face and they flew into the side of the tent. A rush of wind blew through the area as the tent peg outside was ripped out of the ground by the force of the person landing. Tent material swirled around them, covering everyone inside.

"The reflective surface!" someone called out. Their bodies moved about, struggling with the fallen fabric.

Jayla was already tearing at the tent material, her hands clawed and pale. She ripped through, only to scream in pain.

THE SUN!!

Its streaming rays jolted her like painful jade splinters.

THE MOUNTAINS! HURRY!

"No!" Basala cried out. "We 'ave to stop 'er. By nighttime she'll stay turned!"

Jayla, nearly blinded by the brightness, raced to the safety of the mountains behind the marketplace. She took one last whiff of the food she wanted, but pain drove her to fly deep into the coolness of the mountain, her body completely transformed into the grim-shu, as wispy and uncatchable as the wind.

Jayla was gone.

CHAPTER 16

Excitement grew in Ashlee's chest. Could this be a way to return to Iyah? "Wait, you can connect to the jade world through the arch?"

The Gemstone woman finished dismounting the lysar, wobbling a bit as her feet touched the ground. "The 'jade world?' If you are referring to the Jade Kingdom, it is the same as our world, only on the other side of the Diamond Mountains."

"But you can travel there, through the arch?"

"I cannot, no. I have not found a way to enter the darkness. But the creatures who exist inside the void can bring someone into my castle, if that someone has entered the archway. That is how they brought your friend, here," she said, nodding to Yir, who'd unwrapped herself from Ashlee's shoulder and flitted around the stables. "They found her inside the blackness."

Ashlee felt her excitement waver, but she wouldn't give up on the idea. There had to be a way she and Yir could use the archway to return to Iyah. That way Yir could go home and Ashlee could return to Earth. Or at least get to Iyah and see Bekk.

Loneliness struck her. She existed literally worlds away from any other human. *At least Yir is here,* she said. But it gave her little comfort. She hadn't once thought about what might happen if she remained here, like Bekk in Iyah. And the Gemstone woman—she'd lived here for 3,000 years without any family, never revealing the truth of her isolation. What a lonely existence.

Ashlee peered up at the majestic woman and cocked her head. "I just realized something. I don't even know what to call you."

The woman laughed. "I suppose that is true. I did not offer a proper introduction. My name is Gemna."

"Is that like...Queen Gemna or Lady Gemna or something?"

Gemna paused before answering. "Truthfully, I am Empress. That is what my people call me. But I would prefer if you were to call me Gemna."

Ashlee smiled. "Will do." They entered the castle, the Jadari popping out of small jade portions of the walls.

"What is it?" Gemna asked, weariness in her tone. Ashlee didn't think Gemna was tired of the Jadari, but after all the riding and destroying of the grim-shu, she could understand the Gemstone woman's exhaustion, although Ashlee found it odd how fatigued Gemna seemed. She herself didn't feel worn out at all, mostly just sore. But the Gemstone woman appeared to be having a difficult time keeping her eyes open.

The Jadari bounced and gestured. Ashlee tried to follow what appeared to be some sort of ability to convey their needs through bobbing, weaving, and hand motions, but she couldn't figure it out.

"The archway?" Gemna asked.

More movement from the Jadari.

"The creatures brought something new?"

The Jadari headed in the direction of the room with the archway in it.

Gemna took off at a long stride and Ashlee jogged to keep up with her. They ascended the tall steps, though Ashlee felt a bit like she was climbing the side of a mountain instead of a stairway, and turned left instead of right.

"Isn't the archway down here?" Ashlee asked, pointing in the direction of the room where she'd originally arrived.

"No," Gemna said, opening a door. "It's in here."

Feeling a bit confused, Ashlee entered the room behind Gemna. She barely had time to notice the stacks of sparkling books and carving utensils because the archway drew her attention. A creeping sensation crawled up her spine as she stared into the hollowness.

"What is it?" Gemna asked the Jadari.

Ashlee finally noticed what was being referenced. There, on the floor in front of the void, sat a puddle of...she wasn't sure what. It looked like greenish soup with a pearly sheen to it, except it didn't run all over the place like normal liquid would.

Gemna approached the puddle, holding one hand up to indicate that Ashlee should keep her distance. Out of the corner of her eye, Ashlee could see the archway creatures moving inside the inkiness, though she still couldn't quite make out their shapes.

"What is it?" Ashlee asked.

"He has done it," Gemna said, her tone solemn.

"Who has done what?"

Gemna straightened. "The Jade King. He has figured out a way to make the pearly tears work for him. He has controlled someone, but this," she said, indicating the mess on the floor, "is the result of holding a being against their will for too long. I do not know if he did it on purpose or by accident, but either way, he can control others, and it appears he is willing to hold them until death."

The look of horror on Gemna's face made Ashlee's skin tighten. "I take it this is a bad thing?"

The normally lithe and regal woman slumped against the wall. "He has fulfilled the prophecy. He has pierced the void. We are all doomed."

Ashlee gulped. "You got all that from a puddle?"

Gemna hung her head. "You do not understand. The Basalt oracle wrote down the prophecy the first time she came to our castle. My family bound it within a gemstone book, to be kept as a remembrance. When the oracle returned the second time, to show my mother the prophecy through a vision, she brought her daughter, Basaila, with her. It was the daughter's job to make sure her mother made it home after the ordeal, as showing the vision took a huge physical toll. Before they left, they requested to borrow the gemstone book. Basaila said she wanted to study the prophecy and figure out if there may be an alternate way to keep it from happening.

"My family let them take it," Gemna continued, "since they'd been the ones to provide the prophecy originally, but as time moved forward, my family grew restless. As I told you before, they'd planned to move the Jade child, but before they could leave to collect the gemling, the Diamond Mountains went up, the archway opened, and my family died. The gemstone book remained on the Basalt people's side, unreachable because of the Diamond Mountains."

Gemna traced a finger around the edge of the arch, never quite touching it. "I truly believed...foolish of me I suppose."

Ashlee sat down. "What?"

"I thought perhaps Basaila would have been successful in stopping the Jade King. But it appears the prophecy came true. He's broken through the darkness."

Ashlee thought for a moment. "What *exactly* did the prophecy say would happen?"

"That the one who pierces the veil by using the pearly tears would bring peace for both gem and stone and the world would be one again." A crystalline tear formed in the corner of her eye.

A few beats passed as Ashlee wondered what she was missing. "I'm sorry, but...peace doesn't sound like a bad thing to me."

Gemna turned her face, her sapphire eyes boring into Ashlee's. "The Jade King now has access to an infinite number of resources. He will bring peace by destroying my people and taking over our lands with his own. The stone people will find their 'peace' in our obliteration. We will find 'peace' in death."

CHAPTER 17

Jayman stared at the archway, its unnerving darkness unwavering like an endless night. "How will you close it?" he asked.

"I have no idea." Taker Jayro, who'd been touching all around the edges of the archway, had now begun to lightly toss things in the room against the entrance. They all bounced off, as if it were solid. But Jayman could feel...not exactly air...but some sort of energy exuding from it. He knew that if a person moved through that doorway, it would not be a pleasant means of travel.

"All I know is," Taker Jayro went on, "if it is closed, the Jade King cannot return through it."

"Perhaps we could wall it up?"

"We could, as a temporary solution, but walls can be broken down. Eventually, he might return."

"So what if he does? It's his castle."

Taker Jayro swiveled his head to peer over his shoulder. "Have you been living inside a volcanic cave for the past thousand years? Why would you *want* the Jade King to return?"

Jayman crossed his arms, defiant. "As a matter of fact, I just met him a week ago. He seemed quite pleasant. He'd even planned to send his daughter to find out about how the Royal Family could once again earn the trust of their people."

"Was this before or after you and she fled the castle for your lives?" Taker Jayro said with a sneer. "Before or after his guards brought you here and placed you in the dungeon when the king wasn't even here to speak with you?"

Jayman had no answer. He never prided himself on his ability to plan or think—his Beloved had always guided him in that direction. A preference for a simple life appealed to him more than strategy or politics. Owning an inn, giving shelter to travelers, learning how to perfect his iron shakes, these were the types of things that occupied his mind.

"What makes you think preventing the Jade King's return will help?"

"Because I met his daughter."

"I know, I was there. But so what?"

"Princess Jayla is what our kingdom needs. She will lead us with grace and beauty. Using her ability to see our future, she will make sure we are on the right path."

Jayman didn't fail to notice the idolization in his voice. "Perhaps, but Jayla is gone. She's run away. No one knows where she is."

"We'll find her. Somehow. But we need to make sure the Jade King doesn't return in the meantime."

Jayman shook his head. He just wanted to go home. But here he was, stuck in the Jade King's personal chambers of all places with a fanatic bent on changing the whole kingdom in one fell swoop.

Taker Jayro suddenly froze. "Did you hear that?" he whispered.

Jayman strained his ears. Silence. Then...there. A scraping noise. Outside the room.

"I thought you told me these quarters were safe?" Jayman retorted, his voice low.

Taker Jayro waved him quiet. He picked up a book lying on the floor next to the bed, its cover sparkly and bright in a way Jayman had rarely seen before. *It's covered in gemstones...* he thought, amazed. Taker Jayro held the book over his head, ready to bring it down upon whoever entered the room.

Jayman backed up against the area of the wall where they'd entered, sliding down into a crouch next to the bed. He was not a fighter. At least, nothing more than a few scrapes in his youth. He could not stop an assault against trained soldiers. And if Taker Jayro thought a bash with a book would stop the hundreds of guards in this castle, he was insane.

The scraping noise stopped right outside the door. Jayman's eyes widened. He saw Taker Jayro's grip on the book tighten.

Movement inside the arch. Jayman's gaze flickered over towards the inky pit. He couldn't see anything except blackness, but...there. Like a moving shadow inside a cavern.

Before he could say anything to Taker Jayro, the door creaked open. Jayman's attention flew to the new addition in the room.

A shorter, grayer being slid through the entranceway. Jayman made out large, black liquid eyes.

"Wait!" Jayman shouted.

Taker Jayro twisted his arms just in time, the book swiping past the being's face, a gush of air from the movement disturbing the travelling cape around its shoulders.

"Good reflexes," the being said, gently closing the door behind it. "That may come in 'andy."

"I recognize that accent," Taker Jayro said, retreating a step. "Are you from the Basalt people?"

The Basalt woman stepped into the light. "I am, indeed. I've 'eard much about you, Taker Jayro."

Jayman watched Taker Jayro's eyes widen.

"You have?"

"Yes. My aunt let us know about you. She wasn't sure if you'd listen, if you'd 'eed 'er words, but my mother knew, which is why she kept my aunt posted regarding your work for so long."

Jayman didn't understand any of the conversation. He still sat huddled in the corner, not sure how he was seeing a Basalt woman inside the Jade Castle. Had they infiltrated the place? Did they learn the Royal Family was missing and had taken over?

"My lady," Taker Jayro said, bowing with a nod of his head. "It pains me to tell you that your aunt has crumbled, not past a week ago."

The Basalt woman lowered her gaze for a few moments. "She was not long for this world. Tough ol' Night Marble, though."

Jayman finally scooted upwards from his hiding place, body pressed against the wall. The Basalt woman gasped.

"I'm sorry to have startled you," Jayman said.

Her eyes narrowed. "Just wasn't expecting you. What's your place in all this?"

"My-my place?" he stuttered.

"In the prophecy."

"I-I don't have a 'place.' I got arrested by the guards and kept in the dungeon."

"Why?"

"I left the castle with Princess Jayla. The guards came to my inn, thinking she'd be with me. When she wasn't, and when I couldn't tell them where she was, they returned me here." Jayman wasn't sure exactly what made him answer this woman, but she emanated a sense of power he recognized. He'd felt it around the Jade King as well. She was a woman of importance somehow. "Taker Jayro and the Jadari rescued me from my cell and brought me to this room."

The Basalt woman waited a few beats, then nodded, as if calculating the truth in his story. "Very well. It seems you may 'ave been the missing piece."

"Missing piece? To what?"

Before she could answer, they heard it. Rushing thumping footsteps.

"You must go," she hissed at the two men.

Taker Jayro stared at the arch. "I can't. Not until this is sealed."

"Fool. It cannot be sealed. It *must not* be sealed. The prophecy needs to be fulfilled." She pointed at the wall where Jayman stood and, surprisingly enough, Taker Jayro moved towards it without any resistance.

"Ah," she said. "Good. The book."

Jayman peered down at Taker Jayro's hands, which still carried the tome.

A smash sounded against the door. Jayman jumped. The guards were here!

"The Jadari will take you," she said to Taker Jayro. "Give the book to the Jade ruler. It is the only way to bring peace."

"I don't understand," Taker Jayro said.

"Go. Now!"

Jayman watched in awe as she began to change. A glow came from within her and she turned a strange pearly white.

The door slammed open.

Jayman felt the familiar pull of the wall, but this time he didn't resist. He wanted more than anything to exit the room.

The Basalt woman's eyes met Jayman's. *Tell Basala about Jayla.* The words resounded inside his head, as if she'd yelled them in his ear, yet her mouth never moved.

The guards grabbed the Basalt woman.

"No!" Taker Jayro cried out.

Before Jayman's face was pulled backwards into the wall, he saw the Basalt woman reach out with one fingertip and touch the inside of the arch.

A bright light.

Then only the sucking darkness of traveling...

CHAPTER 18

Four hours had gone by since the girl, Belle, had run away and his guards had mysteriously melted. Creaks and groans of the castle being slowly converted to jade around him did nothing except amplify the silence.

He'd failed.

Three thousand years of work for nothing.

After Belle had run off, the Jade King attempted to touch the greenish puddle of one of his guards, to use the pearly substance inside him to...to what? Bring her to life again? Command the substance to rise? He'd then moved to the throne, attempting to use its power to do the same, but to no avail. The globs of melted guards around the entrance to the room could no longer assist him.

So he'd simply sat and stared into space, not really seeing anything.

But then a thought slid its way into his mind. In his own world, he'd crossed through the archway and ended up here. Since he couldn't go through a doorway because he didn't have the life energy of a fairy, perhaps he could let someone know how to enter the arch in the jade world and come here.

Using the power of the throne, he brought forth a doorway to his own world.

Seeing his home struck within him a pang of homesickness. He could have the doorway show him anywhere he wanted: the castle's stables, the edge of the Jade Volcano, the northern reaches near Jayal Village. He inserted the doorway in the midst of busy pubs or children's classrooms. Shouts, waves, and pounding made no difference. No one could see the doorway on the jade world side. No one could hear him yell. And he could not hear them either. Only a view of his home, but no real connection.

Frustration overcoming him, he finally settled on the view of his own room. A mixture of longing and comfort invaded his body at the sight of his own bed and the picture of his family on the wall.

How could he have come this far only to lose? He'd done everything the prophecy requested of him. Sacrificed his own energy, time with his family, sleep, food, even staying to watch his son's body burn just to get through the arch into Iyah. But he could do *nothing* here.

Movement occurred through the doorway inside his room.

No doubt a guard doing rounds or a Jadari cleaning the accumulation of dust and ash while I'm away.

But it wasn't either. Instead, two men came out of the wall next to his bed.

The Jade King straightened and stood stock still, peering through the archway. *Who are they?*

Rage surged inside the Jade King. How *dare* someone enter his personal chambers! And where were the guards? How could this be allowed to happen?

The Jade King strained his eyes, not wanting to miss a single moment. Once again, he could not hear anything, so he merely watched.

One of the men came near the arch, but never quite touched it, his face a mystery to the Jade King. But in the background, another man stayed further away. The Jade King stared. A sense of recognition washed over him, but he couldn't quite place the—

"Aw, come on!"

The Jade King whirled around at the voice behind him. His body calmed when he recognized the intruder.

"You."

Belle let out a sigh. "Yeah, me. And you. Again." She threw up her arms and raised her head, peering up at the ceiling. "Why do you want me here? What am I supposed to do?"

The Jade King tilted his head, watching her. "Who are you speaking to?" he asked.

Belle returned her gaze to the Jade King. "I don't know. Iyah, I guess."

Understanding rolled over him. "You are not in control of your fate here."

She clicked her tongue against the roof of her mouth. "Looks like."

Though he still did not always understand the way she spoke, he was beginning to recognize what she meant by her words.

A thought rumbled in his mind. "What happened to you when

you left this room? Did you see any more of my guards? There should have been some stationed outside the castle."

"I didn't get outside the castle," she said. "I got to some...I don't even know what to call it. The entryway? It was like a million doors overlappin' a million other doors. And then I woke up."

The Jade King's ears perked up. "Woke up?"

She nodded. "That's how I return to my own world. I'm asleep there. When I wake up, I'm home. When I fall asleep, no matter how much I want to *not* be in the castle, I'm here again."

The Jade King pondered this new information. Is that why he did not slumber in this place? Was it a way in and out of other worlds, but once here, that means of escape did not exist? He let out a sigh. Just another way he could not leave.

Belle pointed at the doorway behind him. "What's goin' on there? What is that?"

The Jade King turned around, having completely forgotten that he'd been watching the happenings in his room. He'd missed everything that had occurred. "No," he muttered. The two men were both leaning against the wall next to his bed. One of them held...something? The room began to grow brighter and he couldn't see the men anymore. A light flooded the room from the right side, overtaking the space. The doorway's frame began to shake.

The Jade King moved away. "Stand back!" he told her. Belle moved away towards the throne, standing next to it, gripping its arm.

Cracks started to form *inside* the doorway.

What is happening? he thought, panic flooding his chest.

The light grew brighter, shining outwards now, into the throne room. A figure formed, silhouetted in the brightness, and yet the Jade King could see the tell-tale darkness of the archway as well. Somehow it existed simultaneously inside the doorway.

"Who are you?" the Jade King demanded.

The form took shape. Shorter and stockier than the Jade King, but not as small as Belle. Darker in color, like an ash storm. Liquid eyes opened. A gasp emerged from its mouth.

A Basalt woman.

Shock hit him. She'd managed to break through from the archway in his world and into Iyah.

All thought of the prophecy, of his goals, of his destiny fled from his mind. He only had a single thought: to return home.

Desperate, the Jade King charged the door, convinced if she stood inside and held it open, he could break through into his world.

Right before he made contact, he skidded to a halt as the Basalt woman held up a hand and spoke. "I see it clearly now. I understand, Mother." She peered into the Jade King's eyes. "She used you. When the Gemstone Royals failed, she knew you would pursue this world for your own selfish needs and so the prophecy would still be thwarted." The light surged through her, creating more cracks in the frame, cracks within her own skin. The Jade King recognized the scene: the same thing happened when the oracle came to see him, right before she died.

"I have questions," he said, reaching out to touch her. "Please, do not leave me here alone."

"The true king of Iyah is coming..."

Shock hit him. What was she saying?

"Wait..." He touched the doorway's surface.

A force like a boulder slammed into him, knocking him backwards. He crashed into the base of the throne.

He heard Belle scream.

The light brightened even more. The Jade King shielded his eyes. A warm pulse of air blew over him.

Then, silence.

The Jade King uncovered his face. The doorway remained, with no trace of the archway, but it did not look the same. It appeared to be...broken. Cracks wriggled themselves across its surface. The edges seemed to be crumbled with age. The image of his home remained, but a feeling of nothingness came over him when he stared into the space.

Standing slowly, he limped to the entranceway, studying it for a moment. He wanted to talk things over with someone, work out what had just happened.

"I suppose you have questions," he said to Belle, turning to face her.

Belle was gone.

A slight glow emanated then faded from the arm of the throne where she'd been holding on. An imprint of her body, like a blackened smudge stretched across the wall where she'd last stood, was all that remained of her.

The Jade King stood alone once more, the last words of the Basalt woman running through his head.

"The true king of Iyah is coming..."

CHAPTER 19

Panic. Pure panic.

Bekk kicked as hard as he could, struggling to swim as fast as possible. He'd just rounded the area where the firestream met with the Eclipse Sea when he saw it: a purplish haze moving towards him from the west. It swept across the surface of the water, moving slowly, like an oncoming storm. But Bekk knew the weather patterns of Iyah. This appeared...unnatural. It didn't fit.

It's another part of Iyah closing over this one!

Several fairies flew overhead, cheering him on in his mind as they waited for him to reach the shore. Finally, out of breath and sopping wet, he slid onto the beach. Huffing and puffing he sat up and faced the oncoming haze.

No malicious intent seemed to exist, just a constant movement towards him.

King Fai landed next to him on the sand, his purple body almost the same color as the haze.

What is happening? King Fai asked.

"I think the areas of this world are colliding," Bekk answered, pushing himself up to his feet. He did some quick calculations. Three different areas had been spotted moving over the fairy realm, from the east in the forest, from the south at the Sugar Caves, and now from the west. Bekk only had one recourse: to move northeast towards Yar Castle and the Jade King's location.

More fairies arrived, having heard the call to meet at the beach. They stared at him with their small faces, their bat-like wings moving steadily while they hovered. They wanted him to tell them what to do.

Bekk had no idea.

Vic had disappeared hours ago during their run, right before they'd reached the Eclipse Sea, so he couldn't even ask his friend. He was alone, again.

Then a voice sounded in his mind.

Bekk, I'm here!

Bekk looked skyward to the north and saw Ryf flying to meet him, her golden body shining. A sense of relief washed over him.

"Ryf!" he cried out. She landed next to him on a piece of washed up doh-iyah tree and hugged his leg.

Oh Bekk, it's true. I heard about the other places moving into ours and I went north to check. It is happening there, too. A green globby mass moving over the Tarana Caves, this way towards us.

"Well, that settles it. Every place is converging towards the castle." Bekk shook his head. "We'll have to go there."

The fairies all fluttered and tittered. King Fai spoke up. *Bekk, we cannot. The Jade King wishes to use our life force to open the doorways to other worlds, just like He did before. I will not let the fairies suffer again.*

Bekk rubbed his face, remembering how his brother had done the same thing to the fairies previously. "I know. I know. I don't want that either. But we can't survive in these other realms of Iyah. If we don't head in the direction of the castle, we won't make it anyway." He paused. "Maybe that's why the Jade King did this? To get us to come to him? His guards couldn't catch us..." Bekk looked around. "Speaking of, has anyone seen any of the soldiers lately?"

The fairies all shook their heads. One fairy, a pale silver, spoke up tentatively. *One melted.*

Bekk stared at her. "Melted? What do you mean?"

Suddenly, Bekk heard someone calling out his name. He turned to face the voice and saw Vic in the distance, running towards their group from the edge of the forest. Bekk waved, so happy to see his friend. However, Vic had barely crossed half the space when he popped out of existence again.

Bekk let out a frustrated grunt. *Okay,* he told himself, *you can't depend on Vic or Belle coming to help you. You can do this.*

"Sorry. You were saying about the soldier melting?"

The little silver fairy flapped her wings a bit faster, looking uncomfortable with all the other fairies staring at her. *Y-yes,* she stuttered. *One came out of the Sunbeam Forest and reached for me. I flitted away, but then when I looked again, its eyes looked strange. They weren't white anymore, but alive and normal, and it let out a terrible noise, like it was in pain. Then, it, well, it became liquid and sat as a puddle on the ground.*

"On stone?"

No, on soil. But the thick water didn't sink into the ground. It just...lay there.

"Did anyone else see something like this? Or see any of these puddles?"

A few murmurs raced through the group and several of the fairies nodded, having remembered strange greenish pools of liquid on the ground.

"What does this mean?" Bekk asked. He faced the sea and stared at the haze still coming. Regrouping, he told everyone, "Regardless, we need to move towards the castle. If the soldiers are somehow gone, maybe we can hide near the Golden Trees until we can figure out what to do. Also, continue to keep an eye out for guards or any more of those puddles." Ryf called out an order and a few fairies flew a little further ahead to scout. The rest of them moved forward once again.

Ryf fluttered near Bekk's head. *I'm scared, Bekk.*

"I am too, Ryf," he mumbled. Somehow, when he'd made the decision to stay in Iyah and thwart his brother a month ago, the decision had been so quick he'd barely had time to register what he'd done. Now, during what would be a half a day's march to the castle, he felt like he would be hiking for hours towards the end of his existence. And sentencing all the fairies to the same possible fate.

While walking, Bekk went over the few things Vic had relayed to him from his brother about Iyah. There had to be something in those details to help him and the fairies defeat the Jade King and restore Iyah.

"Okay," he said out loud. "Maybe you can help me out, Ryf."

I will do my best.

"Shon said the throne holds the power to open the doors to other worlds, but only the power from the fairies allows passage through them."

Our crystals.

"Or, your life energy, which is what I think the Jade King believes is the only way to do it. That's why he told my brother to kill the fairies, to get their life energy."

That was a scary time.

"Yeah." Bekk blew his hair off his sweaty forehead. He'd already dried from his swim and the sun overhead shone with a ferocity he wasn't used to. "But, that means the Jade King hasn't gotten through any of the doors, correct? Because his soldiers haven't caught any of you."

That makes sense.

"So going towards the castle is bringing him what he wants."

I think so.

Bekk let out a sigh and slowed a bit. "Does that mean we are playing right into his hands? Is he somehow making Iyah collapse in on itself to drive us to the castle?"

I don't know. Yir would know. She was always the cleverest of the fairies. I miss her.

"I know you do. I'm really sorry we don't know what happened to her. At least we know she's somewhere because she visited Ashlee in a dream."

Saying Ashlee's name caused a dull ache to form in his chest.

He hadn't expected to fall so hard for her, especially after their rocky beginning. And then to lose her just when he'd finally gotten to know her?

"Focus," he told himself, shaking his head to clear it. "Okay. Shon wrote down that the arch worked like a gateway between the stone world and here, a gateway that wasn't created by the throne. But once it *was* created on the stone side, Shon could open it using the throne's power, just like any other door. Except..." he paused here and swallowed. "The only way to open the archway on this side was to want to die."

Bekk wondered about that. He definitely didn't *think* he wanted to die, so he didn't know how he could open the archway to push the Jade King through. "There has to be another way."

I'm sure there is. Keep talking. We will find it.

A large dip on the meadow's floor indicated to Bekk that there were about three hours left of their walk to reach the castle. He glanced behind him to check on the progress of the purple haze. It was still advancing, but it looked like it hadn't quite reached the shoreline, so at their current pace, they were still moving faster than its boundary. This helped relax him quite a bit.

"Yeah, sorry, keep talking. We know Belle keeps being put near the Jade King, so maybe there's a way for me to give Vic a message to send to Belle, so she can tell the Jade King that he doesn't have to *kill* the fairies to get through the doorways. He just needs their crystals. Maybe then he'll stop what he's doing and...and what? We let him win? Go through doorways and start wars and conquer places? That won't work either!" Bekk kicked at a pebble on the ground. "Besides, I can't count on Vic. Last time I saw him he was only here for a few minutes running through the forest towards us."

Ryf fluttered. *Actually, he'd been here for quite a while. One of the other fairies found him lost in the forest on the wrong side of the firestream. She helped him find a way across and then he caught up with us but then he disappeared again.*

Bekk took a moment to digest her quick words. "He was here for a while?"

She nodded.

"I wonder why Iyah put him so far away from me? Does that mean he might return somewhere in the forest again? We can't leave him alone, not with the world collapsing."

I'll send a few fairies to keep an eye out for him. Don't worry. We won't let you lose your friend, too.

Bekk gave a weak smile. "Thanks, Ryf. Make sure no one ventures too far away. And tell them to continue to keep an eye out for soldiers, just in case."

Right before Ryf was about to speed away, Vic appeared so suddenly and right in front of Bekk that Bekk smashed into him. They tumbled together to the ground.

"Vic!" Bekk exclaimed, grappling him into a hug in the grass. "You're back! You're here!"

"Ow." Vic's face pinched in pain.

"Oh, sorry man." Bekk pulled away and helped Vic to his feet. His friend rubbed his shoulder, rotating it a bit with a grimace on his face.

"I didn't see you. You just appeared."

"It's okay. I'm okay."

Bekk noted the hollowness in Vic's tone.

"What's going on? I just saw you a few hours ago, running towards the beach, but then you disappeared."

"I didn't want to come." Vic marched a few feet away and hollered into the sky. "I *told* you I didn't want to be here anymore! Not until you let her go!"

A chill raced through Bekk's spine even through the heat. "What are you talking about?" He grabbed his friend by the shoulders and faced him.

Tears welled up in Vic's eyes. "It's Belle. She's in a coma, too, just like Ashlee."

CHAPTER 20

Ashlee stood, absorbing what Gemna had just told her. Peace from the Jade King's point of view meant the annihilation of the Gemstone people and the conquering of their lands. No wonder Gemna's family were so intent on halting the prophecy.

The idea that she currently resided in a world where at any moment she could be obliterated along with everyone else here struck her. A sense of fear churned in her belly. She didn't want to be in this place anymore.

Ashlee stared at the archway, watching the shadowy creatures move around out of the corner of her eye. "You said you've been asking these arch creatures to bring you someone from the other side. That, at first, they told you about someone who looked like they were made of jade and sitting on a throne. You thought that was the Jade King, right?"

"That is correct."

Ashlee couldn't help but notice the detachment in Gemna's voice. This latest revelation seemed to have wiped her of any remaining hope. Well perhaps there was another way this situation could be approached.

"But the creatures couldn't get the man on the throne. They brought Yir instead."

"Yes."

Ashlee studied her little flying friend. "Why?"

Gemna's eyes, which had glazed over a bit, cleared. "Why what?"

"Why didn't they bring you the man on the throne?"

"They could not."

"Why not? Was he too big? Too heavy?"

Gemna frowned slightly. "I don't know. I never asked."

"Could you ask now?"

"To what end?"

Ashlee forced the anxiety in her stomach to keep at bay while she spoke. "If the Jade King is there, now, maybe the creatures can bring him here. You can, I don't know, put him in a cell or something."

A flicker of movement crossed Gemna's face. "I had not thought of that. I only focused on pulling in someone who could tell me what the Jade King's plan was, someone on his side, helping him, but I never thought about the source himself." She took a seat in front of the arch, her back straight, her arms relaxed at her sides. Ashlee moved to get a better view and saw Gemna had closed her eyes. Her lips moved, but no sound came out.

Ashlee shifted her gaze once again to the archway. She could still tell there was movement, but couldn't make out specific shapes. As she watched, the movement increased.

Several minutes later, Gemna opened her eyes, her face contemplative.

"What did they say?" Ashlee asked.

"They said they only bring those that are at an end. The Jade King has not arrived yet." She paused. "I'm not sure what that means."

Ashlee ran over the words in her head. They stirred something inside her mind, someone else's words from what seemed like a lifetime ago.

"Shon," she whispered.

"Excuse me?"

"Oh, sorry. I was just thinking out loud." Ashlee chewed her bottom lip. "I suppose I might as well tell you. I knew someone who could call the archway wherever he wanted it to appear. But he said the first time it showed up, it was because he wanted to die. He said...he said the archway is a portal to the world of the dead."

Gemna peered at the archway as if seeing it for the first time. "That explains a lot. The creatures have only ever brought me dead or dying beings. Until your fairy friend, that is. And then yourself."

"Right..." Ashlee glanced over at Yir. "Yir, could you come over here for a minute?"

Yir fluttered nearby and landed on the edge of the bed. *Yes, Ashlee. What is it?*

"When you came here, you started in Iyah, right?"

Yep. I miss it.

Ashlee gave a soft smile. "I know you miss it. I'm trying to get you home. But this is important. You told me He was killing fairies.

That He'd caught you and then you felt you were...floating?"

Yir nodded. *Yes! Then these dark creatures grabbed me and took me and I ended up in the room with the long table.*

Ashlee thought about that. When she, herself, had arrived, she'd entered from the archway into Gemna's bedroom. But Yir arrived and came out in the dining room. And now they were staring at the archway in what appeared to be a study. "Gemna, does the archway move?"

"No. It exists here only."

"But Yir and I didn't come through the arch into this room. We arrived in other rooms."

Gemna's forehead furrowed. "What?"

"Yeah. I arrived in your bedroom, where I found Yir in the crystal container. And she told me she showed up in the dining hall."

A look of surprise crossed Gemna's face. "I assumed you'd both emerged here and wandered into the castle. So other archways are able to open and deposit someone inside other rooms?"

"It seems like it."

"Hm. I cannot imagine the Jadari would not have been aware of any new additions to my castle, but if someone came through without my knowledge..."

"Would it matter?" Ashlee asked. "You said they always come dead. Until Yir. And me." She paused. "Ah, I see. If Yir and I got through alive, maybe someone else did, too."

A Jadari popped up, as if Gemna had called for it, even though no one said a word.

"Just who I'd hope to see," Gemna said. "Tell me, have there been any other intruders since the archway arrived?"

The Jadari shook its head.

"Are you sure? Would you know?"

Hand and head movements followed. Gemna then said, "They say they can always feel a change in the castle. It is immediate, like a new stone being placed on a pile. They can feel the weight, the size, all of it." She made a noise of surprise. "I never knew how sensitive they are."

"Just in case," Ashlee said to Gemna, "not that I'm doubting anyone," she noted to the Jadari, "but could you ask the arch creatures how many beings they've brought forth through the archway?"

Gemna communed with the creatures. "Five."

Ashlee wrinkled her brow. "Well, there's Yir and I..."

"And the melted being before us."

"That's three. The fourth and fifth?"

Gemna's eyes widened. "I...I do not know." She spoke with the Jadari once more. "Right now!?" Gemna rose from the floor. The tone of alarm made the hairs on Ashlee's arms stand up.

"Someone else is here?"

"Two someone's apparently. Lead me," she told the Jadari. She threw her cloak over her shoulder and stalked out of the room behind the small, green being.

Ashlee followed closely behind, indicating for Yir to stay nearby. They moved through corridors quite quickly, Ashlee jogging a few times to keep up. They took the other staircase this time, instead of the one which led to the stables, and it deposited them near the front doors.

There, Ashlee saw the outline of an archway imploding, just like she'd seen it do after she'd arrived in this world.

On the floor in front of it lay a pile of dark grayish rocks shaped a bit like a body and a mound of a person next to it.

The mound didn't appear to be made of stone.

Ashlee's heart caught in her throat. It couldn't be...

She rushed ahead past Gemna.

"Wait!" Gemna cried out. "It could be a trick!"

But Ashlee didn't obey. She slid on the gemstone floor, ignoring the pain in her knees from the motion. With bated breath she turned the body over.

It was Belle.

CHAPTER 21

Jayman couldn't breathe. And yet, he didn't seem to need to at the same time. The darkness around him, crushing him from all sides, also felt comforting and protective.

He didn't know how long he existed in this state, between danger and safety. It could have been seconds or days. All sense of time fled from him. He only existed moment to moment, still himself, and yet part of his surroundings.

A light touched his eyes. Air moved against his skin.

"Breathe," he heard a voice say. "Just breathe, luv."

Slowly, Jayman took in a breath. Then another. His eyesight cleared. He stood in a small cottage, but didn't recognize his surroundings. Not just because he'd never been here before, but because everything appeared different. Craggy rock made up the walls, instead of the smooth jade he'd normally see. The ceiling hung low and curved overhead as opposed to the high vaulted ceilings of most of the Jade Kingdom's inhabitants.

"Where am I?" he muttered, the words thick in his mouth.

"You're in my 'ome, in Bajay Village," the woman replied.

"You're safe. The Jadari brought you 'ere. Do you remember?"

Jayman nodded slowly, the recollections flooding into him. He could picture the Jade King's room, the archway, the Basalt woman turning to light, her words screaming inside his mind...

Clarity hit him. "I'm supposed to speak with Basala." The remnants of his travels faded and he focused on the person in front of him. Another Basalt woman. "Are you Basala?"

She smiled. "No, dear, 'e is out. Should return tomorrow, though." She led him to sit at a small table. "Walling with the Jadari always makes us 'ungry. I'll get you something to eat while you regain your wits." She scurried off to the kitchen. He could hear the sounds of cooking implements being moved around.

At that moment Jayman realized the cottage only contained himself and this woman.

"Excuse me," he said over the clatter, "but where is my companion? Where is Taker Jayro?"

"You arrived alone, dear," she said, hustling over to the table. She placed a plate and bowl in front of him, the first steaming, the second sloshing. "Was someone supposed to be with you?"

"Yes." Jayman frowned. "Why isn't he here? We left the castle together."

The woman paused. "The castle? What castle?"

"The Jade Castle." His stomach growled and he automatically dug into the food.

The Basalt woman sat down across from him. "I'm sorry, but you only just arrived by your lonesome. If there was another, I 'avent' seen 'im."

Jayman paused mid-chew. "You don't seem surprised, though, that I'm here."

"Basaila told me a Jade man would be coming." She nodded at the wall behind him and he turned to glance at it. "We made that wall out of jade for the Jadari to travel. Basaila went through it to go to the Jade Castle. She said to expect you." Jayman returned his gaze to the woman. "I would'a thought she'd 'ave returned with you. Did she tell you she planned to stay for some reason?"

Jayman swallowed his bite, the food scraping his throat as it tightened. He remembered her body turning into a bright light... "I'm, uh, I don't think she's coming."

"Why not?"

"Well...I'm not really sure how to tell you this, but she may have been captured by the guards." He paused, remembering the light, the way she'd touched the archway. "Or...she may not have made it."

"What does that mean?"

He shook his head, his chest suddenly tight. "I'm sorry. I don't really know what's going on myself. She brightened, like a white light, and the guards grabbed her, but then she touched a doorway, so maybe she went through it?" He shook his head again. "I know I'm not being very helpful."

The Basalt woman's eyes narrowed for a moment, but then softened. "Basaila warned me that 'er journey would be treacherous. Even with all 'er gifts, she could not predict 'er own fate."

The woman's words rang inside Jayman's head. "Predict? As in the future?"

The Basalt woman gave a curt nod, picking up the empty dishes from the table. Jayman hadn't even realized he'd completely finished the food. "Basaila was an oracle."

That word. That was the word used by Taker Jayro about the Basalt woman he'd worked with in the hospital. And about Jayla.

"I've heard that term before, about someone else. *Two* someone's actually."

The woman focused on him. "You 'ave? About 'oo?"

"The man I was supposed to be traveling with, Taker Jayro, he worked at, well sort of like a hospital, for people who have problems with their minds."

"The M.A.G.M.A. Institute. Ay, we know it well. Even throughout our 'ardships with the Jade people, they 'ave always allowed anyone with Basalt 'eritage to come to the 'ospital for 'elp. In fact, Basaila's aunt 'ad gone there, decades and decades ago. Didn't make no sense to me. She seemed right as ash rain."

"Taker Jayro spoke about her, too," he said, struggling to remember. A yawn escaped his mouth. It was as if traveling through the jade wall and into this new territory had sapped him of all his strength and mental capacity. He wondered briefly if there were any other more serious side effects. He knew that only Jadari traveled that way. It couldn't be healthy for others to do so, could it?

Jayman wanted nothing more than to return home and sleep in his own bed, but how long would it take before the castle guards realized he'd escaped from the castle's dungeon and retrieve him? Besides, he had no way to travel to the inn, unless the Jadari transported him again, but it seemed they needed a specific type of jade wall to do so. No area in his own establishment looked like that.

Too many new thoughts and questions. A throb began right behind his eyes. He yawned once more.

"I'm terribly sorry," he muttered, "but I can't seem to stay awake."

"Walling will do that to you, too," she said, already guiding him to a small room in the rear of the house. "You'll feel much better in the morn."

"Someone should let my Beloved know I'm all right," he said, lying down on the flat bed. It felt a bit spongier than the beds he was used to, but it didn't take him long to adjust.

"We'll send a message out, I promise. I won't reveal where you are though, to keep 'er safe. This whole mess is like a runaway mokaki herd, completely out of control." She pulled over a black heat lava lamp and turned it on, the soothing warmth making him even more drowsy.

"There's something else," he mumbled, his eyes already closed.

"What's that, dear?"

"I'm supposed to tell Basala about Jayla. Basaila told me so."

"Shh," she said. "We already know all about 'er. She'll return tomorrow with Basala and then all three of you can speak to each other. We'll get this straightened out, I promise."

The Basalt woman left the room, closing the door gently behind her. Jayman let his body sink into the bed as all the events of the past few days fluttered through his mind. Eventually, they overlapped one another like a background of white noise and he felt himself drifting away into sleep.

Right before he succumbed, he heard a new voice through the closed door in the other room. A man's voice.

"A message arrived for you from Basala in Bagem," the man said.

"What 'appened?" the Basalt woman asked.

"Message reads: 'It's about Jayla. She turned and then she flew into the mountain. She's gone.'"

A moment passed. "Then all is lost..."

CHAPTER 22

The darkness and coolness of the mountain soothed the grim-shu's wounds.

It didn't like this place. It didn't belong here. It wished it were home.

But the inside of the mountain felt *close* to home.

It could stay here and live until it figured out a way to return.

It remembered the first of the grim-shu that entered this new world. All grim-shu were connected through their *mai-so*, a spirit-like essence that gave them life. Because of this, they could all tap into one another's knowledge and feelings, yet remain individuals as well. It created a harmony among them the grim-shu had grown to rely on.

Then the looming dark space appeared, arched and blacker than the inside of any dwelling. It caught a grim-shu and pulled it away from its home and into this world, into light and heat and pain.

All grim-shu back home felt that pain and cried out.

The grim-shu on this new world found what the creatures here called a "mountain." The insides reminded the grim-shu a bit of home: unbroken density packed together, coolness, and absolute darkness.

But after a while, hunger grew inside the first grim-shu, intensifying with every passing moment. The creatures of this world smelled delicious. They also possessed their own type of *mai-so,* but it remained contained inside a single body, without connecting to those around it. The grim-shu fed and it felt sated, drinking the new *mai-so* from its prey, replenishing itself. The beings here tasted like nothing the grim-shu had ever eaten before.

However an unexpected consequence occurred. A new grim-shu was born from the remains of the hollowed-out body, still appearing like the eaten being, but now existing as pure energy and reconnected through the *mai-so* to the grim-shu.

The two of them created more grim-shu in this manner, feeding and living happily, creating a new community, until a creature made of shining dense material shone a light on one of them when it came out to feed.

The bond to that grim-shu was broken. That grim-shu faded from existence.

It pained the whole collective. But what could they do? They could not return home. They did not know how. And the hunger... the hunger always drove them forward.

It was this same hunger that tugged at the insides of the current grim-shu.

It still hadn't eaten. But the brightness and the warmth hurt.

It could control itself. It would not venture out for a meal.

Another hunger pang.

Willpower did not seem to matter. It would need to hunt.

Moving slowly, the grim-shu tested the edges of the mountain, nearest the outside. Where it felt heat from the brightness that shone down from a large orb upon this strange world, it shied away.

Testing methodically, searching as the hunger twisted and moaned inside its intangible body, it finally found a portion that did not feel as warm, that did not seem as bright.

Waiting impatiently, the grim-shu moved through the stone of the mountain and tested the outside.

Still too bright.

Still too warm.

Over and over it tested.

There. Darkness had fallen over the land. Heat had disappeared.

It squiggled through the mountain's edge and peered around. Dark mushy material covered the sky, blocking the large orb that wanted to shine.

It wasn't sure how much time it had. But movement nearby caught its eye. A troupe of creatures ambled along, carrying long staffs and shiny stones in pails. Their *mai-so* radiated from their skin, their flesh. They were walking away from the mountain's base, heading towards a group of dwellings in the distance, their tiny lights causing dots of pain in the grim-shu's eyes.

Nevertheless, this was its moment. If it were going to feed, it must do it now, before the workers returned to their homes.

The grim-shu slithered down the hill, staying incorporeal. It knew it did not have to materialize until it fed.

Closer, closer it moved, its body trembling with anticipation. Gliding along the very top of the ground, it closed in upon its first meal.

"GRIM-SHU!"

The scream echoed across the rocky valley and the creatures turned to face their attacker. Tiny lights in their hands shone up at it, hurting the grim-shu's eyes. It turned away, but the pain was not as bad as before. It could withstand this. If only it could eat, it would have the strength to combat these tiny lights.

It would retreat a bit, come around from another angle. A way the grim-shu had never tried before.

From below.

Down it dove. It would bide its time, popping in and out of the earth beneath its prey so it could regenerate and heal from the light's pain. The creatures above circled each other, backs against one another, holding up the lights.

No grim-shu had ever come up from the ground before. They always retreated into the mountains, to safety. But this grim-shu would be cleverer. It would wait until they began to walk again, when their guard was down, and sneak in from underneath.

The urge to eat gnawed at its insides, but this time the grim-shu knew it could wait just a little while longer for the meal it would have.

Then it could sense a connection through the *mai-so*—two other grim-shu nearby, hiding inside the mountain.

A feast, it thought to them. *Come. We will trap them and feed...*

CHAPTER 23

"Oh my God, BELLE!!" Ashlee swooped over her friend. She drew on what she remembered learning about basic CPR and leaned over Belle's body, listening for breath.

It was there.

With trembling fingers she searched for a pulse. It beat, steady and sure.

A shuddering sigh of relief escaped Ashlee's mouth. "She's alive!"

"Who is she?" Gemna asked, peering over at the new addition to the room.

"A friend of mine. From home." Ashlee gently shook her friend, but Belle's eyes remained closed. "She's not waking up." Ashlee whipped her head towards Gemna, panic in her chest. "Did your creatures bring her here because she is about to die?"

Gemna spoke with the creatures inside the arch. "No. They said she was not who they'd grabbed. The Basalt woman had come through the archway. Your friend was..." she paused, as if asking the creatures to clarify. "...added to their bounty through energy."

Gemna shook her head. "I'm not sure what that means either, but I think it means she wasn't who they'd planned to bring. And that she's not dead or dying."

"Then why won't she wake up?"

"Again, I am not sure. Perhaps she needs time? Perhaps she suffered a shock to her system."

Ashlee cradled her friend's head in her hands, tears welling up in her eyes. She couldn't believe how good it felt to be with someone from Earth again. Even though she'd only been in this world for a day, it felt like the longest day ever.

"Well, once again, if she can get here without dying, maybe we can all return home."

Gemna was about to answer when a Jadari burst through the wall near them, signaling wildly.

"Another one?" Gemna's voice sounded both afraid and exhausted at the same time. "Meet me at the stables. I will go immediately."

"What is it?" Ashlee asked. "Another body?" Images of Bekk or Vic flew through her mind.

"No. Another grim-shu. This one straight east, in the town of Gemru. I must leave."

"What about my friend?"

Gemna paused in the doorway, her sapphire eyes dull. "You may stay with her if you'd like. The Jadari will take care of you both." She leaned against the wall, her body slumping slightly.

Ashlee didn't feel like she'd be much help against another grim-shu and she didn't want to leave Belle alone, but something stirred at her inside. The woman in front of her was completely depleted.

"Are you all right?" Ashlee asked.

"I..yes I am fine." Gemna gripped the frame of the doorway. "I just...usually I rest after a grim-shu attack. It is very taxing. Most sightings are decades apart. There have never been two attacks in one day before."

"Are you sure you can handle it?"

"I will have to. The grim-shu can devour a gemstone individual in an hour, a whole village in a day."

"Can't someone else work the diamond-light thingy?"

"Of course. But I have never shown anyone else how to do it. It would take some time to learn."

Ashlee bit her lower lip. "Time like a lysar ride out to the village?"

Gemna's eyes showed recognition. "You would do that? Stop a grim-shu?"

Ashlee looked down at Belle's unconscious body. "If I want to get us home, I'm going to need your help to do it. I can't do that if you are asleep or so worn out you can't function. You can teach me on the ride and then get some rest on the return trip."

A look of admiration crossed Gemna's face. "I am impressed by your courage."

"Don't be," she said, clasping her shaking hands together. "I'm scared out of my mind. But even I know something is wrong. I'm not supposed to be here and neither are Belle or Yir. That has to do with the archway and you're the only one who can communicate with the creatures inside it. I need you and I know you won't let your people die."

Gemna nodded. "Then let us go. You have time on the ride to change your mind, of course. It will take about half the travel time as the trip this morning. I will not force you to do this task. It is not difficult, but it is...draining."

Ashlee swallowed, hard. "I understand."

"And your friend?"

Ashlee glanced at Yir. "Will you stay with Belle and the Jadari so she sees someone she recognizes if she wakes up?" She paused. "Well, she'll recognize a fairy, not you exactly."

Of course! But Belle won't be able to understand me.

"I'll leave a note." She furrowed her eyebrows. "Do you have a pen and paper in this world?"

"We have items to write, if that's what you're implying, but we must move quickly." Gemna retrieved something from a shelf and placed a strange contraption over Ashlee's finger. It reminded Ashlee of some sort of emerald thimble, except pointed at the end. Fitting a little loosely, the contraption contracted to the correct size. A blank slate lay in front of her.

"Etch onto the slate," Gemna instructed.

Ashlee used her finger, delighted when green lettering appeared on the page. She quickly explained what was going on and that she'd return soon.

"Let us go," Gemna said, urgency in her voice.

"I'll be back as soon as I can," Ashlee told Yir, giving her a hug. Then she followed Gemna out of the room, jogging to keep up.

They arrived at the stables in a short period of time, mounted a lysar, and took off straight east. While they rode, Gemna retrieved the diamond and lamp and held them in front of Ashlee.

She spoke first about the diamond. "It is difficult to see without proper lighting, but this diamond has a crack in the middle of it. Because of this, when the light is placed behind it, it shines through in a prismatic fashion. This allows the light to split across the area, streaming outward. When these rays hit against any reflective surface, they create a sort of 'web of light' to trap the grim-shu."

"Sounds simple enough."

"Aiming the diamond is a bit tricky, but you'll sense how it is supposed to move."

Ashlee held the diamond, turning it over in her hand. It almost took up the space of her whole palm. She couldn't even imagine its value on Earth. "Sense?"

"This is the tricky part. Whatever force created the diamond mountains gave them...well...a life of their own. They aren't sentient, not like you or me, but they...react to things. They react to other life."

"In what way?"

"They draw on it."

Ashlee frowned. "What does that mean?"

"The day my family crumbled, the diamond mountains formed. I believe that their life essences were used to create the barrier. Because of this, the mountains will absorb other life energy. I believe—now this is just a theory—that the grim-shu who live inside are what currently feed the mountains. This is why I believe the mountains are spreading, because they are growing while they feed off the grim-shu's life force."

Suddenly, the diamond felt heavy and warm in Ashlee's hand. "Wait, is this thing sucking the life out of me?" She had the sudden urge to throw it.

"No, it is not life energy, it is energy in general. But the grim-shu exist as pure energy in their translucent form. The more energy from the creatures the mountains consume, the hungrier a grim-shu feels to replenish the loss."

"But that won't happen to me, because I'm solid?"

"Yes. The use of the diamond consumes energy, which is why, as you've seen, I feel fatigued afterwards. But we are made of more than pure energy, so we are not losing our life force, not like the grim-shu."

"How did you learn all this?"

"Not every grim-shu has died. In the beginning, I left the diamond at the first village where it was found. When another grim-shu showed up at a different village, I used an alternate diamond, which only trapped the creature by the light, but did not kill it. Kept from feeding, it eventually faded away. Before it died, it spoke, begging for food, talking about its home. It broke my heart. That's why I took over possession of the original diamond prism. I bring it to each village and I use it whenever I can, to promote a quicker end."

"That sounds pretty harsh either way."

A somberness tinted her words. "I cannot help them return home, but I cannot let them feed on my people. I have worked for many centuries with many others to find another way, an alternate food source, anything to help them return to their world, but we have failed. And because their numbers grow on the other side of the mountains, the mountains grow over here, covering our world."

Ashlee always knew she wanted to help others. Ever since her family acquired a lot of money, she'd planned to use those funds to assist people who had more need when she became an adult. But this woman had the weight of an entire people and land on her shoulders. She had no family to depend on, no friends to consult with. Ashlee was reminded of those leaders in history who stood up and fought, even against overwhelming odds, because they cared about their countries and their people.

Now, sitting here in a strange world, she didn't know if she could help. Fear raced through her at the thought of holding an energy-draining diamond in her hand to kill a creature that simply wanted to go home.

She knew she didn't have to. She could relinquish the task over to Gemna.

Either way, she needed to decide quickly. A town came into view at the edge of the horizon, the tiny lights shining in the evening's overcast dimness.

"Is that it?" she asked.

"Yes. The town of Gemru. One of the first towns ever constructed in the Gemstone Dominion. It used to be a trading post with the Basalt Territory, until the mountains rose."

"Why do they still live so close to the mountains if they are no longer trading and have to deal with grim-shu attacks?"

"They are one of the frontline villages. This is one of the areas where the Diamond Mountains encroach the fastest. I believe it is because the grim-shu are more popular here. Why? I couldn't say, but Gemru has the best rate of keeping the mountains at bay. Unfortunately, they also have the highest number of grim-shu attacks. They are truly brave to stay and fight."

Ashlee watched as the village became clearer. Their lamps barely shone against the sides of the buildings and off the roads. She compared the town to the last place they'd visited and noticed she could see more of the color red, even amidst the darkening sky. *Rubies,* she thought. *This place must be made mainly from rubies.*

Her heartbeat sped up as the lysar slowed. Shrieks could already be heard, even from this distance.

"Where are they?" she heard Gemna mutter under her breath. The Gemstone woman directed the lysar to move around the northern side of the village, getting closer to the mountains.

"There!" Ashlee called out, pointing. She could see a circle of about a dozen individuals, their reddish-colored skin flashing here and there in the weak beams of their lava lights.

"Why aren't they headed towards the village, towards the lights?" Gemna asked out loud.

Ashlee strained to watch their movement. If nothing else, they seemed to be creeping closer to the mountains. Then she saw it. A translucent being emerged out of the ground between the villagers and their homes, forcing them to retreat towards the rocky base. They shone their lights at it and it sunk once again beneath the ground, but immediately another one appeared, still between them and their houses, but a bit further south. The lights shifted again, forcing it back down.

"There's more than one," Ashlee said, the wind whipping her face as the lysar picked up speed to reach their target faster.

Gemna said nothing, but Ashlee could feel the pressure from the Gemstone woman's arm tighten across her chest.

One of the villagers spotted their arrival and pointed. The others waved their arms in the now darkness, merely sparkly silhouettes.

Suddenly the lysar reared up and veered to the left. A grim-shu had sprung up from the ground in front of it. It smelled of ocean air, fishy and salty at the same time. Ashlee barely had time to notice its face, similar to the Basalt person she'd seen from the first grim-shu attack.

Without thinking, Ashlee held up the lava light. It shone full upon the creature, and she could see it had materialized, its mouth wide to bite the lysar. It immediately turned translucent in the brightness and retreated, but in those same few moments, Ashlee felt her body flying through the air from the lysar's quick movements. Unmounted, she fell with a *thud* to the ground, her right elbow and knee sending up sharp signals of pain. She heard the groan of Gemna landing next to her.

Ashlee stood quickly, adjusting the lamp in her hand to ward off any more attacks, when the shrieks of the people began again. The grim-shu, three in total, were surrounding them.

With a turn, Ashlee reached down and shook Gemna. "Get up! Hurry!"

But Gemna didn't move.

Oh no, oh no, oh no.

Ashlee froze for a moment, her feet cemented to the ground, her eyes wide as she stared at the circle of soon-to-be food.

Nothing in her life could have prepared her for this moment. Not her parents, with their busy hours and more care for money than spending time with her, nor her siblings, who'd all moved on in their own lives, nor her other classmates, whose fears revolved around getting into college or talking to a cute boy.

Then she thought of Bekk. He'd faced a choice like this over four months ago and chose to sacrifice his own life to stay in Iyah. He'd confronted his brother and left everything he knew, everything he cared about, to save a place where he didn't even belong.

A warmth spread through her. She pictured him with her, now, encouraging her, his hands on her shoulders, her face.

You can do this, she imagined him saying.

Without giving herself the chance to think her way out of the situation, Ashlee made her legs move. One of the villagers lay on the ground, the others hovering around him. She forced herself not to look at him, to see if any damage had been done. She didn't want to see anything that might scare her out of the task at hand.

"Where is Empress Gemna?" one of them cried out, shying a bit away from Ashlee. "And who are you?"

"I'm here to help," Ashlee said, her voice shaky. She held up the diamond to the lava lamp, like Gemna had instructed. The light bounced and spread all over the area. The grim-shu all retreated under the ground. It wouldn't keep them away forever, but the circle of prismatic light would at least keep them scattered for a bit.

"Get your mirrors ready," Ashlee continued.

"There are three of them!" a younger woman yelled. "We can't escape!"

"It'll be okay," Ashlee said, feeling foolish and small amongst these towering people. "Gem-, uh Empress Gemna told me what to do."

Though many of them didn't appear relieved, they did assemble into a looser circle, holding their mirrors facing one another.

Ashlee shook her head. "That won't work. We'll never get all three together inside the circle at once." She thought quickly. "We'll have to make a line, slightly curved at the ends, and angle the mirrors mostly at the ground. I'll then bounce the light off them. They won't be able to stay under the ground for too long because of the light. When they pop up, we'll corral the grim-shu like cattle, and push them towards the mountains."

"Corral them like what?"

"Oh, sorry, um like lysar."

The villagers followed her instructions and Ashlee let out a shaky breath. Once they'd assembled, she turned her light towards them. The glow increased exponentially and flashed against the ground. Ashlee could hear hissing noises and two of the grim-shu rose, immediately retreating towards the mountain.

"It's working!" one of the villagers cried out.

*Only two...*Ashlee thought, her eyes flicking around in their sockets. *Where's the third?*

There. Movement behind the line, near the fallen body.

"TURN!" Ashlee yelled.

The line whipped around, holding their mirrors. But before Ashlee could shine the prismatic diamond, something happened. The grim-shu had stopped, transfixed on its own image in the mirrors.

Ashlee felt a hand grab her shoulder and she whirled around. Gemna stood there, a tar-like substance trickling from her temple.

"Kill it," she ordered.

"Wait!" Ashlee pleaded, facing the grim-shu.

Gemna wrestled with the diamond. "Hurry, before it escapes!"

"No! Something is happening," Ashlee said, grunting with each word as they fought for the diamond. Ashlee, though, was no match for the woman's strength and tough skin.

Ashlee saw out of the corner of her eye that the grim-shu had reached out to touch its own reflection. Without any thought, Ashlee flung herself between the light and the grim-shu, blocking it from the harmful rays. She watched, her heart in her throat, as the grim-shu began to transform. The ambient light showed soft features, unlike the blocky appearance and gray skin of the Basalt woman. She seemed smoother, and greener, like turquoise or...

...or jade, Ashlee realized.

The woman completed her transformation and collapsed to the ground.

Ashlee rushed over to the fallen woman. She touched her hard, smooth skin. Movement. Her eyes fluttered open for a moment.

Breath came from her mouth.

"She's alive!" Ashlee shouted.

All the villagers crowded around until Gemna pushed through. She stood there, her face a mask.

"She's a Jade woman," one of the villagers whispered.

Gemna gasped and dropped the lamp and diamond to the ground with a crash. "She is more than that." Ice coated her words as she pointed at the woman's arm. "She is a Royal."

Ashlee peered down to make out some sort of mark, then glanced up at Gemna. The darkness in the Gemstone woman's eyes and the tautness of her face caught Ashlee off guard.

"What should we do, Empress?" one of the villagers asked.

With clipped words, Gemna said, "I will return her to the castle. Since she is Jade Royalty, she will pay for the crimes of her family." She reached down, grabbed the unconscious woman by the arm, and dragged her to the waiting lysar.

"What?" Ashlee said, following her. "You can't do that. You don't even know if this woman has anything to do with the Jade King."

Gemna remained silent, ignoring Ashlee's words.

"Please, Gemna, don't do this. Not until you talk to her. She is a source to find out what's going on in the Jade Kingdom. Please." Ashlee grasped at anything that might stop Gemna's vengeance. "She survived being a grim-shu as well. No one has ever done that. It may help you save others in the future."

"Perhaps she sacrificed herself to become grim-shu to wipe us out," Gemna replied, acid in her tone.

Ashlee shook her head. "You don't believe that."

Gemna whipped around. "How dare you attempt to decipher my thoughts and feelings? You, who come from another world." Her sapphire eyes narrowed. "Perhaps you were planted here to make me soften so the extermination of my people will go easier."

Ashlee's mouth dropped open. She had no response. Gemna had crossed over into ravings. There was nothing to say that would help.

Maybe the ride will calm her down, Ashlee thought. *I'll try talking to her again once we return to the castle.*

They reached the lysar moments later and Gemna draped the Jade woman through it. She settled herself in as well. Ashlee made a move to join her.

Gemna glared at her. "This is where we part ways. I must tend to the prisoner without you clouding my judgement. I will not have my land conquered!"

"B-but what about Belle? And Yir? How are we all supposed to get home?"

"That is no longer my concern. If your friend wakes up, I will send her and your fairy to this village. You are no longer welcome at my castle."

Before Ashlee could protest further, Gemna urged the lysar to ride away.

CHAPTER 24

Shon stood in the activities room, his focus far from the painting he'd been assigned to work on. Slants of sunlight streamed through the slatted blinds, casting lined shadows across his easel. Other patients worked around him, swiping watercolors across their canvases, following the instructions to paint "how you feel today."

The last he'd heard from Belle or Vic had been two days ago when they'd come to visit him. He'd hoped they would've called today, since Belle said she would update him, but he supposed they were busy with school and the like and he may have to wait until the coming weekend for another meetup. Or perhaps they hadn't been able to return to Iyah and so there wasn't any new news? Or even worse, what if Ashlee hadn't woken up from her coma and passed away and Belle and Vic were now dealing with another friend's funeral?

His gaze roamed the art room. He could tell, even during his down days, he still felt better than usual. The doctors noticed as well. Once again, Dr. Nancy Romal suggested he may be able to leave in-patient treatment.

"We would still be in contact of course," she reassured him, "until you feel more confident about the transition. But I really think you're ready."

Was he ready? All he really knew was that he couldn't help his brother while stuck in this place. So, Shon stayed positive through all the therapy one-on-ones, did all his chores, talked about the things he looked forward to on the outside in group sessions, even if they were lies—like his girlfriend, his brother's friends, and other members of his family. He spoke of returning to school and getting a job again. About missing cooking. Anything to appease the staff.

Shon knew his doctor was discussing him right now with the higher-ups. He also knew that the other reason for the "push" to get him out was that the state only required three months of full-time care after Bekk's death and almost five months had passed. Someone had to be paying for all this, but Shon wasn't sure who. Whoever it was—insurance or the government—he was sure they didn't want to spend money on him for any longer than necessary. Either that or he'd have a hell of a bill when he got out.

In the middle of his wandering thoughts, Shon noticed a newspaper on the table near the paintbrushes. Normally he didn't pay much attention to the outside world, but since he may be immersed in it soon, he figured he could see if there'd been any major wars or new political leanings that had popped up in the last few months.

Shon froze. The headline on the open page sat above two pictures of young women—young women he recognized as Ashlee and Belle. The headline read: MYSTERIOUS COMA CLAIMS

TWO MONROE H.S. STUDENTS.

Shon noticed the art therapist moving around the class and when he faced away to comment on someone's painting, Shon reached out and snatched the paper. He quickly skimmed the article.

Ashlee Andiers, age 16, fell into a coma three days ago on Saturday morning, found by her friends during a sleepover. Normally this reporter wouldn't think much of it, except one of the friends who found her, Belle Minton, age 16, suffered the same condition two days later. Both young ladies are at Saint Clara's Hospital, monitored closely by doctors. Is this a drug interaction gone wrong? A virus? A prank that got out of control? Should you be worried for your own teenagers? This reporter will keep you updated.

Shon stood for a moment in shock, then noticed the instructor on the move again, so he tossed the paper once again onto the table and resumed his painting.

First Ashlee, now Belle. Iyah had claimed someone else. But why? What was happening to these girls in their dreams to keep them trapped in that world?

Frustration mounted inside him. Once again, he felt helpless. He couldn't visit anyone, he couldn't return to Iyah to find out what was happening, and he couldn't talk to anyone about it.

A glimmer of hope rose in his chest at the sight of Dr. Romal. She approached him with even steps and a wide grin.

Could it be? Was he really going to be released?

The doctor motioned for Shon to join her, giving a nod first to the teacher. Shon moved over, leaving his random brush strokes to dry on the canvas.

"Shon, I have wonderful news. Your release went through without a hitch! I've contacted your grandmother and she said she'll be happy to pick you up tomorrow morning. You'll be staying with her, of course, until you find your own place. I just couldn't wait to let you know."

Shon's heart pounded. He was surprised the doctor couldn't hear it. "That's great, really great. I mean, I'm nervous, but I'm excited to get to my life again."

Dr. Romal placed a reassuring hand on his shoulder and squeezed. "Just remember, take it one step at a time. And we'll still be in touch. I'll have the receptionist schedule our first follow-up session for later this week. But congratulations, Shon. You've worked hard and you deserve this."

She gave one last smile, turned, and trotted off.

Tomorrow, Shon thought. *One more day and I can go visit Vic, find out what's going on, and see how I can help get those girls back into this world.*

CHAPTER 25

A numbness rocked Bekk backwards onto his heels. "What? No. What? Belle is in a coma, too?"

Vic rubbed his eye with his fist. "Last time I was here I got dumped in the forest. I planned to tell you Belle was with the Jade King again. She saw his soldiers melt away at his feet. The Jade King didn't understand what was going on either. He can't get through the doors, he can't go home. He's stuck here, by himself. He doesn't know what to do. She thought maybe she could talk to him, let him know we could help him get home, if he opted to stay there. Solve all this peacefully."

Bekk took in all this information, forcing his brain to process everything through the shock. "Ah, they melted. Yeah, I saw a green puddle. That could be one of the soldiers. And I had the same thought, that Belle could pass a message to the Jade King. So, what happened?"

"So we went back to sleep two nights ago, this plan in place. I woke up in the forest and couldn't find you to tell you all this. The fairies guided me. Then, I saw you on the beach, but before I could get to you, I woke up to someone screaming. It was Belle's mom."

A tightness formed in Bekk's gut. "Because of Belle?"

Vic nodded, his forehead taut. "Yeah. She came to wake Belle up, she does that every morning. I've been sleeping on the floor, cuz we have to be together to come to Iyah."

"But when Belle didn't wake..."

"Exactly. Her mom came into the room when Belle didn't respond, then screamed. That woke *me* up and I sat up and she screamed again at seeing me there."

"What did she say?"

"I have no idea! I got the hell out of there, going through the window."

Bekk nudged his friend so that the two of them would continue to walk. "You bolted?"

"Yeah. I mean, a teenage guy lying next to her daughter's bed when her daughter won't wake up? Couldn't imagine that would go over well."

"Doesn't she know you and Belle are dating?"

"She met me like once last year. I don't know if she knows we're still together." He rubbed his face again. "This is such a mess."

Bekk thought quickly, wanting to reassure his friend, but also get more information. "Okay, it's probably not that bad. What happened next?"

"I wanted to go home, but I got worried they might send the cops. So I crashed at my friend's dorm at the college I go to. I've stayed with him before when I've had a big assignment so it wasn't a huge deal." He glanced around. "When I fell asleep last night, I thought for sure I wouldn't end up here again. I mean, we never came here when we slept by ourselves. That's why I kept staying in Belle's room."

"Well what are you going to do when you wake up?"

Vic's voice shook. "I don't know. All I know is I'm not waking up until we find Belle. I'm going to that castle to get her. That way if she's fine, I'll be fine, and everything will return to normal. So where's the castle?"

"We're heading right towards it." Bekk's mouth felt dry as he realized the implication of Vic's word: *if* Belle was fine. That placed two girls he cared about in comas. What if neither of them ever woke up in the real world? What if they died here, just to save Bekk?

Vic stopped in his tracks. "Wait. I thought the castle was the last place you'd want to go."

"It is, but I, we," he said, waving his hand to encompass the fairies, "don't have a choice. Iyah is collapsing on itself and all signs point to the castle being the main focal point."

"Meaning?"

"Meaning we have to go there or we'll die."

Vic puffed out his chest. "Well I'm going to take out the Jade King or whoever for whatever he's done to Belle. She said he's trapped here, which means he can't get away."

"How are you going to stop him? He's a giant guy made out of stone."

"I don't know, but there's gotta be a way."

The two friends trudged in silence for a short while. Bekk did his best to keep his panicky thoughts at bay. He had to keep hoping a solution would present itself, somehow. After several minutes, they could see the outline of the castle on the horizon.

"How long until we get there?" Vic asked.

"Not long. About an hour." Bekk tried to ignore the lump in his throat. They needed a plan. They needed a weapon. They needed *something*.

But what could two teenagers and a bunch of fairies do to stop anyone? Bekk remembered how strong his brother had been, wrapped in jade, almost fully comprised out of it. Except this king *was* made out of that stone. They'd need a cannon or jackhammer to do any damage. They didn't have anything like that.

Bekk could hear Vic mumbling under his breath next to him, but whether he was thinking out loud about ways to stop the Jade King or simply keeping his anger going to fuel himself to move forward, Bekk couldn't tell.

Stop focusing on Vic. Come on, Bekk, you can do this. You have to know a way to stop him.

Suddenly, a voice sounded inside his mind. Unlike the fairies who spoke at a normal level, this voice boomed inside his skull. Bekk fell to his knees, hands clutching the sides of his head.

"Arrghh," he cried out in pain. He could feel Vic's hands on his shoulders, see Ryf's face hovering below his.

Almost as soon as it began, it stopped. The quiet of both the valley and his friend's voices took him a moment to get used to.

"Bekk, are you okay, man? Can you hear me?"

Bekk gave a weak wave. "Yeah, yeah I'm all right." He allowed Vic to help him to his feet.

"What just happened?"

"I heard a voice. A booming voice, in my head."

Vic's eyes widened in fear. "Was it the Jade King?"

"No." Bekk ran a shaky hand through his hair. "It was my brother."

Vic took a beat. "*Shon?* You could hear him? What did he say?"

"He said 'Remember the JadeSlagger. Picture it. Then, emerge. Use the throne.'"

"Remember the what? What the hell is a JadeSlagger?"

Bekk shrugged. "I have no idea. I've never heard of it be—" The word trailed off as a memory entered his mind.

"What is it?" Vic asked.

"He said 'Use the throne.'"

"Yeah? So?"

"So when I found my brother here, there was a creature, a huge creature that came from the jade around the doorway. I think...I think that's a JadeSlagger."

"How can you be sure?"

"Because I destroyed the thing when I touched the throne and called out for the chair's energy to protect me. I think..." Hope welled up inside him. "I think Shon is trying to tell me that I can create the creature by picturing it and calling for it to 'emerge' and stop the Jade King."

A few beats passed and then Vic shot his fist into the air and whooped. "Oh, man, this is seriously maxxed! We have a way to beat him!"

Ryf, who'd been fluttering nearby, spoke to him. *Bekk, the other realms of Iyah are still coming.*

Bekk wrenched his head to check over his shoulder. Sure enough, the purple haze had covered the entire sea edge and was coming across the meadow floor.

"We gotta keep moving," Bekk said, picking up his pace again. Adrenaline shot through his system.

"Not a problem," Vic said, a grin on his face.

Though the warmth of hope burned inside him, Bekk still felt a sense of dread lingering in the recesses of his mind. The castle grew larger and clearer as they approached it. He veered a bit to the south, heading towards the golden doh-iyah tree cluster at the edge of the Crystalline Valley.

"Where are you going?" Vic asked.

"The fairies need to stay here, hidden. We can't afford to lose even one of them to the Jade King. They'll be safe among the trees." The sense of dread continued, but Bekk couldn't quite place the problem. With this new information from his brother and a safe place for the fairies and the guards out of the way, there shouldn't be a problem confronting the Jade King, right?

Except...except how could they get to the throne to use it? If the Jade King was there, wouldn't *he* use the throne first and stop them?

The golden trunks rose up in front of them and they quickly moved into the copse of trees.

"Ryf, let the fairies all know to stay here, no matter what. If the other realms of Iyah get too close, use your crystals to enter the front door, focus on a world, and enter it."

Leave Iyah?

"It's the only way you'll survive."

We will not survive outside of Iyah.

Bekk stared at her. "What do you mean? There are millions of other worlds you can go to. I'm sure one of them will support fairy life. You just have to focus on it. The throne will be active so its energy will help you do that."

King Fai, with his plump purple body, settled next to Ryf on a nearby branch. *We appreciate all you have done as the true leader of Iyah, but this is where we exist. The throne's energy created us, long ago. Without its presence, we will no longer be.*

"What are they saying?" Vic asked.

"They're saying they can't leave Iyah. If the realms collide and the throne is destroyed, they will all die."

"Holy crap," Vic said under his breath. He then shook his head and exhaled loudly. "Well, guess we'll have to save them as well as Belle and Ashlee."

Bekk felt the thump of Vic's hand on his shoulder.

"You ready, man?"

The sense of dread finally revealed itself to Bekk. "Not quite." He turned to Ryf. "I'll need you to come with us."

What for?

"What for?" Vic asked at the same time.

He didn't want to say it. He wanted to believe he and Vic could do this on their own. But he knew there was only one way the Jade King would leave the throne. One thing he would want more than anything else...

"We'll need Ryf as bait."

CHAPTER 26

The Jade King wanted to throw something, but no items existed in the room except the throne and the darkened chandeliers that hung above, out of reach.

The Basalt woman's words echoed inside his skull, the only sound except his heavy breathing and his footsteps as he paced.

"*She used you. She knew you would pursue this world for your own selfish needs... The true king of Iyah is coming...*"

A fury, like boiling lava, filled him. How *dare* that oracle from so long ago use him for her own needs. And to what end? To get him here? Make him lose his son and daughter in this apparently pointless pursuit? Keep him trapped here, unable to leave, unable to effect change?

"No," he growled out loud. "I won't let her win."

But what could he do? He had no guards to help him, no way home. Even that young lady, Belle, annoying as she may have been, did not return after her encounter with the Basalt woman. Only a shadowy smear remained, the only proof she'd ever been here at all. That he hadn't just imagined her to sate his loneliness.

The Jade King stood behind the throne at the top of the short staircase, pacing, his fingertips never leaving the top of the chair. He could do this. He could figure a way out. He would *not* be used. The oracle may have sent him here under her own guises, but he would prevail.

The Jade King paused for a moment, staring out of the castle's large windows. He could see across the landscape, over a valley of what appeared to be some sort of crystalline pebbles, and into a stand of tall, golden...well, he wasn't sure what they were. They didn't have anything like these huge still creatures in the Jade Kingdom. Were they friendly? Foe?

After staring for quite some time, he came to realize the golden creatures did not move. They remained rooted, like mountains in the soil, even though their tops swayed in the breeze.

Perhaps they are not creatures, but this world's equivalent to our mountains, he thought.

Movement.

The Jade King held his breath. He tightened his eyes, straining.

There it was again. Tiny jewels that sparkled in the green sunlight. They flittered around inside the tall golden rocks.

"Fairies..." he whispered. A longing rose from his gut to his throat. He only needed one of them and he could break through into another world. He could bring new guards through, come up with a better way to catch the wily flying creatures, and fulfill his plan.

No one makes a fool out of me, he thought. *I will make this prophecy my own!*

But how? How to catch one of them? He couldn't leave the

castle. The multi-doored room frightened him.

"I need something..." he mumbled out loud. "Something to catch one of them..."

An energy surged into his fingertips via the connection to the throne. Intrigued, the Jade King peered downwards and watched green energy flow into his hands. It stung and tickled at the same time. The energy pulsated and stretched out into the space, creating a new world inside the doorway the Jade King didn't recognize. A dim, silent room. Curtains hung over the windows. A young man slept in a bed, tossing and turning. The man appeared similar in shape and color to Belle.

The Jade King peered closer. He almost felt like he recognized the young man. Yes, he knew him, his puppet from before. But why was the throne showing him this image?

Suddenly the young man sat up, eyes wide. Though the Jade King couldn't hear anything, he recognized the word mouthed by the man.

YOU.

Just as suddenly, the young man's eyes rolled upwards into his head and he again fell onto the bed. Then, the energy of the throne leapt to the man, connecting to his head. From this connection, a shape emerged and slithered through the doorway towards the Jade King.

The Jade King snatched his hands away from the throne, severing the connection, but was too late. A creature formed and sat there, a strange mix of jeweled tones and rocky exterior. A long, sharp stinger of jade hovered behind it.

"What are you?" the Jade King demanded.

I serve.

The words rung inside the Jade King's head. He shook it, as if clearing away ashes floating into his face.

"Did you speak?" he asked.

Yes. I serve.

The Jade King paused. He had somehow drawn this creature from the mind of that young man in another world. Did this mean the throne could bring things, creatures, even others through the doorway and into Iyah?

Before he could contemplate what this could mean, the creature's head snapped towards the windows.

Someone approaches.

The Jade King, still a bit leery, followed its gaze. Indeed, three creatures approached the castle from the golden statues. Two looked like Belle, though male, and one much darker in tone, and a golden fairy hovered near their heads.

Why were they coming to the castle? Was it to surrender? A peace talk? Belle had spoken about how she thought she was supposed to help him. But had she been a ploy sent to catch him off guard, test his weaknesses, gather information to report to her companions?

Well he would not be tricked. He would not be used again.

"Can you capture a fairy for me? Alive?" he asked the creature.

Yes.

With that one word, the creature scuttled off towards the door.

A sense of hollowness stole through the Jade King. He had no idea what he'd just sent after the fairies. But at this point, he couldn't seem to care...

Instead, he shifted his view once again out the window.

Watching the three individuals come closer to the castle.

Closer to helping him win...

CHAPTER 27

It took several moments for Jayman to open his eyes. They felt heavy and dry. Finally, after rubbing them fiercely, they widened, revealing a room he couldn't place.

At last he remembered. He rested inside a Basalt woman's home.

A flash of panic stole through him. He had been charged with telling Basaila about Jayla, but instead he'd fallen asleep.

Wrestling himself off the bed, he left the small bedroom and entered into a common area. The Basalt woman who'd greeted him the night before was scurrying to and fro around the room, shuffling stone slabs, cooking food, and packing all at the same time.

"What's all the commotion?" he asked, his voice hoarse.

She paused, picked up a cup of something, and shoved it into his hands. "Drink," she ordered.

He followed her demand. As soon as the liquid hit his dry throat, it felt soothed. He spoke again. "What is happening?"

"The news 'as reached us, even way out 'ere." She stopped moving long enough to brush some soot from her hands. "We got a notice. The Jade King is gone from Jade Castle. The Marbles are claiming it and storming it as we speak."

Shock hit him. "What? The Marbles?"

She nodded and continued moving around, shoving items into bags and rearranging more stone pages.

"How? When?"

"You've been asleep for almost the whole night. The sun will crest soon."

Jayman sunk down onto a nearby chair. "Why didn't you wake me?"

"I tried. You wouldn't wake. I didn't know if you ever would and I couldn't spend time waiting to see if it 'appened."

Jayman caught the edge of her arm as she moved past him. Terror clenched his gut. "Please," he said when she stopped. "Please explain things to me."

A sharp breath streamed from her mouth, but then her eyes softened and she gave a light nod. "I'll need to be brief. Gotta prepare."

"Prepare for what? What about me?"

"Let me just tell you, dear, then you'll know everything." She sat across from him at the small table. "It appears your Taker Jayro 'as been busy while you've been recovering. I don't know why 'e stayed awake while you slept, but walling affects different people in different ways."

"What did he do?"

"'E spread the word about 'is time in the castle, with you. 'E told everyone about 'ow the Jade King 'ad disappeared to another land, 'ow 'is son was dead, and 'ow 'is daughter 'ad fled. 'E spoke about rallying behind Jayla, about 'ow she was now the true 'eir to the throne."

"Well that makes sense. Without the king or prince around, Princess Jayla should inherit the kingdom."

"Except there's a problem with that."

"What is it?"

The Basalt woman clucked her tongue against the roof of her mouth. "Well, it 'appens that the man you were charged to see and speak to, Basala?"

"Yeah?"

"'E and Jayla traveled to a village near the edge of the Diamond Mountains."

Jayman involuntarily shuddered. He'd never been close to the mountains, but he'd always hated them. Even though their arrival ended the war, their unnatural nature disturbed him. He liked things he could see and feel, things that made sense, that he could understand. Mountains growing up in mere moments did not make sense.

"Why'd they go there?"

"Because when Jayla escaped the castle, she was 'elped to go under the Onyx Mountains." She waved away his question. "I won't tell you 'ow, trade secret, so don't ask. Any'oo, along the way, she was infected by a grim-shu."

Jayman frowned at the colloquial word. "A mountain wraith?"

The Basalt woman confirmed his question with a nod.

The uncomfortableness in his gut spread through his body like a chill from a magma-virus fever. "But mountain wraith infections can be cured, right?"

"Quite easily. If properly 'andled. Unfortunately for Jayla, things went wrong. They administered the anti-infection poultice, but she fled before they could show 'er 'er reflection."

"Fled where?"

"Into the Diamond Mountains."

Jayman slumped backwards. "So she's gone. Consumed by the wraith..."

"Yes. And then Basala with 'is yapping maw goes and tells everyone about 'oo she really is and that all is lost!" The Basalt woman stood with a huff and busied herself again.

"So what?"

"So what? So it means that your friend told everyone the Jade Castle is vacant and Basala told everyone Jayla is a grim-shu! There is no claim to the throne. So the Marbles claimed it."

"But surely there must be *someone* who would take over next? An advisor or council member?"

The Basalt woman shoveled more clothing into a bag. "If there is, no one is making any claim. Rumors floated around, probably by your friend again, that 'alf the guards 'ave also vacated the castle. It's prime picking for the Marbles."

"Then why are you packing? Where are you going?"

"I'm not packing for me, I'm packing to 'elp the refugees going to make their way 'ere."

"Refugees?"

A brusque exhale. "Yes. Don't you know your 'istory? When

the Great War 'appened, the four areas separated even more: Jade, Gemstone, Marble, and Basalt. Since the Basalt Territory lay touching each of the other three areas, many soldiers would cross our lands to get to their enemies' sides. The Marble people, 'owever, were the worst. You know about their focus on military. They 'ad no respect for anyone.

"The Jade King may 'ave been a selfish man," she went on, "but 'e cared about 'elping to fix things after the war. The Overlord of the Marble Realm cares only for 'is own people. 'E 'as been obsessed with finding new areas to occupy. It is why 'e built Marbila Port, to explore the Wastelands beyond the Lava Circle, 'oping to find more territory to in'abit. If 'e claims the Jade Castle, I know one of 'is first goals will be an attack on Basa City, our most southern town, right on the edge where the Pearl River flows from the Diamond Mountains into the Lava Circle. 'E's convinced it's the key to reaching the Gemstone Dominion, no matter 'ow many times we've told 'im it isn't crossable. So I expect there will be many injured fleeing north to seek refuge from 'is reach."

At the end of her rant, she began pulling supplies from the cupboards.

"What about me?" he asked. "Where am I supposed to go?"

"'Ome," she said, a curtness in her voice. "I can't care for you anymore. Your people are on their own."

"I can't return to my inn. The guards are looking for me."

"Since it is known that Jayla was consumed by the grim-shu and the Jade King is gone and Prince Jay is dead, I doubt anyone cares about you anymore."

Jayman couldn't believe how much had changed so quickly. A week ago he'd been running his inn without a care in the world. Now, the Jade Royals were all gone and an invasion was about to happen.

Though he never cared much for studies, he did remember most of what the Basalt woman said about the Marbles. On the whole, they'd always been a very prideful people, but when the new Overlord took power three centuries ago, even Jayman had heard talk of his greed for land. He knew a lot of Marbles weren't happy with the change, but, from what he could recall, there was a long drawn-out process that cemented the Overlord's position. Jayman had known when Jay and Jayla came through with that injured Marble woman, he should have sent them away. But Jay had been one of his closest friends and he'd grown quite fond of Jayla in the short time he'd known her. How could he not have assisted them?

Jayman wondered about the Marble woman. Had she had something to do with the downfall of the Jade Royals? Had she been a spy sent by the Overlord to wreak havoc? Or had she truly been a friend of Jay's, someone he cared about and wanted to help, no matter her origins?

These were questions he'd never have answers to as everyone involved had perished. All he did know, while watching the Basalt woman continue to organize her household items, was that he'd gotten in way over his head. She was right. He should just return to his inn, to his Beloved, and wait to see what happened with the Marbles.

Besides, there was nothing he could do about it.

Thoughts stirred in his mind.

"How did you learn about the Marbles invading?" he asked the Basalt woman.

"Rumors, mostly, from traders."

"Then, have these rumors made it to the Jade Castle, to warn the guards?"

"Not sure. Doubtful if they aren't catering to any outside audiences. It's why I think the Marbles are attacking so fast. Don't want to leave room for chance that anyone could build up a defense."

Jayman's chest thumped. The swirling thoughts turned into an idea, but a crazy one. He couldn't, could he? He wasn't anyone, just an innkeeper. How could he think he could manage the situation?

And yet, look at everything he'd accomplished in the past week. He would have never believed he could help the way he did. Granted, most of the time he'd just been swept up into the situation. This time, he'd be choosing to help. "Do you think..." he began, the fear evident in his words.

"Do I think what? Speak up, speak up, dear."

"Do you think the Jadari could return me to the Jade Castle?"

"Why'dya want to go there again?"

"To alert the guards."

The Basalt woman froze, then craned her neck to stare at him. "Tell me this is a jest."

Even though his body screamed at him to retract his words, he shook his head instead.

The Basalt woman slowly moved towards him and peered

down. He was forcibly reminded of being at school and being scrutinized over an answer he'd given.

"The Jadari will take you, of course. I'm not sure 'ow much good it'll do."

"It won't hurt to try."

"Except you escaped from the dungeon cell. They may just lock you up straight away."

Jayman hadn't thought about that. Fear rushed through his limbs. This was insane. Who did he think he was? He wasn't a hero. He had no clout. And yet, when he thought of his inn, his Beloved, what they would suffer under Marble rule... "Maybe. But maybe they'll listen. I'd rather be in a cell there and have the guards prepared for battle than deal with the Marble Overlord reigning over the Jade Kingdom."

The Basalt woman gave a sharp nod. "Then let's get you moving." She gestured at the wall. A Jadari popped out—still a shock for Jayman to see—and moved its hands and body while the Basalt woman spoke. After several moments, the Basalt woman nodded again.

"All set," she said to Jayman.

A new feeling of unease circulated throughout him at the thought of "walling" again. He wondered if he'd be as tired. He hoped he could stay awake long enough to tell the guards what he knew.

Either way, it was too late now.

Jayman took a deep breath and stood against the wall, body rigid. The same sucking feeling commenced, and he felt himself being drawn into the jade stone behind him.

The Basalt woman stood and watched, her eyes wide. "Good luck," she whispered.

"Thanks," he said, half his head already inside the stone. "And thank you for everything..." He trailed off, realizing in those brief seconds before he completely melted into the wall that he didn't even know her name...

CHAPTER 28

Ashlee stared in shock. "Wait! Please!" she cried out. But Gemna continued to ride away on the lysar, leaving Ashlee to stand alone in the darkness. She'd been abandoned. Whoever the Jade woman was had rocked the Empress to her core, bad enough to leave Ashlee stranded.

Shuffling sounded behind her. The Gemstone people resumed their retreat towards their village.

Should she speak to one of them? Ask for a place to stay? For a ride to the castle?

Before she could make a decision, a wave of exhaustion washed over her. So far in this world she hadn't felt very tired, mostly just sore, although she'd only been here for a day. Now, with the sky darkening and the energy drain from using the diamond to trap the grim-shu, she could barely stand.

She realized at that moment that the diamond lay amongst the broken shards of the lava lamp Gemna had dropped. In her hurry, the Gemstone woman had left it behind. Ashlee quickly picked up and tucked the precious jewel into the pocket of her jeans.

Just in time, too. One of the villagers must have seen her stumble because she rushed over to help.

"Are you all right?" she asked. Her way of speaking sounded similar to Gemna's, though a bit more punctuated on the consonants.

"Tired," Ashlee mumbled.

"Gemala, Gemleen, come here, quick." Two other women rushed over to assist and they moved Ashlee towards the village.

"I need to return to the castle," Ashlee told them.

"What you need is some rest. Then we'll get you where you want to go."

Ashlee's eyes closed and she drifted in and out of a foggy haze. She could hear them speaking above her in hushed tones, wondering who—or what—she was.

"She's a bit pale," one of them said. "Perhaps she's a cross-breed of the Marbles?"

"But she's so small and her skin is so soft."

"A runt of the litter perhaps?"

"How'd she end up here? How'd she cross the Diamond Mountains?"

"Who knows? We can't take any chances. She may be..."

Ashlee didn't hear any other speculative answers as she could no longer focus. She slogged along through a thick murkiness, never quite falling asleep, but not quite awake either.

Several hours later, Ashlee's eyes fully opened. Her whole body ached and she was sure some of it had to do with the flat, hard slab of rock she currently lay upon. The remnants of...whatever state of being she'd just been in rolled over her. She'd been aware of her surroundings, but hadn't been able to move or focus on anything around her. Like being in a coma, but still sensing the room they'd put her in, the fading of the light through the single window, the garbled words of those around her before they left her alone. At one point the room smelled like new asphalt and she noticed a bowl of blackish gunk next to the bed.

When they first placed her in the room, she assumed that if she fell asleep here, she'd wake up on Earth. The idea soothed her and she'd wished for sleep to come. But something kept her right on the edge of that precipice, never quite fully tipping her over. She assumed she couldn't sleep because she wasn't supposed to wake up at home yet.

The notion scared her while she currently sat up on the slab, gently stretching her limbs one by one. A desperate want rushed through her: to return to her cushy bed, see Belle and Vic and her parents again. So why did she still feel like she needed to stay here?

What if I can't *go home?* she thought, the idea crawling through her mind. *What if, like Bekk, I died on Earth somehow and I'm stuck here?* A shiver of fear moved through her, shaking her body, chattering her teeth.

Everything appeared dark and quiet except for the light shining through the windows from the fading moonlight as the horizon lightened. It had a bluish tint to it, unlike the brightness of the moon on Earth. Another pang of homesickness rushed over her.

"Deep breaths," she told herself, remembering what Belle had told her the day at the park when she'd had an anxiety attack. "In and out." She went through the motions and though the fear didn't go away, her body calmed down a bit.

Whatever was going on with her, the answers would not be found here. She needed to return to the castle. Perhaps someone here could take her?

Ashlee rose from the bed and walked towards the door. She placed a hand on the handle and attempted to turn it.

It didn't move.

A new sense of fear hit her. They'd locked her in.

She grabbed the handle with two hands and yanked, but the door remained solidly closed.

What do I do? she thought. *Yell out? Break down the door?* But before she could make a decision, something tugged at her shirt from behind.

Ashlee gasped and whirled around, her heart in her throat. It took her half a moment to realize she needed to look downwards. One of the Jadari stood there, its eyes wide, its face neutral.

"You scared the *crap* out of me!" she hissed in a whisper.

It made some movements.

"I don't understand," she said, shaking her head. "I'm sorry."

It moved towards the window above the bed, turned to look at her, and gestured for her to follow.

"*That* I get." With quiet steps she walked behind it and they crawled through the window and exited the house. She didn't know why she felt the need to stay quiet, but she didn't quite feel safe in this village. Perhaps it was because they'd locked her inside the room where she'd slept. They were probably just as scared of her as she was of them...

That's spiders, she thought with a smile. *Guess it applies to Gemstone beings as well.*

All she did know was that the Jadari lived in Gem Castle, which meant maybe they could help her get there.

Moving across the bumpy landscape, Ashlee crept alongside the small creature. It led her to a rocky area with large jutting crystals and shiny gemstones sticking out of the ground.

"Now what?" she whispered.

They kept moving, walking further down into a cave-like structure. The light dimmed the farther they went and Ashlee froze. "I can't see anything," she told it.

The creature returned and stood next to her. Then the strangest thing happened.

The Jadari began to glow.

Not like a glo-stick or a flashlight, but a soft tinge of green that emanated from inside it. It looked so natural, like a gem lit from within, similar to an exhibit Ashlee had seen at museums in the past. The light was just enough to see the outlines of their surroundings so they could continue on.

For over an hour they moved, Ashlee's throat dry, her feet hurting from blisters. Finally, the cavern began to rise and Ashlee stumbled up into the diminishing nighttime, a vast field of shiny spots twinkling in the moonlight.

A darker area on one of the walls caught her eye. It didn't quite match the sparkling surroundings.

The Jadari approached the dark wall.

"What is that?" Ashlee asked, then shook her head when she remembered the Jadari couldn't answer in a way she'd understand.

The creature merely motioned once again for her to follow. She forced herself to continue on, her body stiff, and stood in front of the wall. It appeared smooth and she ran her fingers over it. A coolness could be felt.

The Jadari stood against the wall and motioned for Ashlee to do the same. Ashlee followed suit. She felt a bit silly, standing with her back against a wall. Why'd she think following the Jadari would help? If her sense of direction was at all correct, they'd moved *away* from the castle this whole time. Maybe the creature...

Something began tugging at her, starting around her hips and butt and Ashlee let out a shriek, wrenching away from the wall.

"What the hell...?" she said, staring at a place on the wall where she'd felt the pull. It appeared solid.

The Jadari pointed at the wall again.

"No way,'" she said. "It's trying to drag me in."

The Jadari made more motions then pointed at the wall again.

Ashlee stood, her body and brain having an internal war. The first wanted her to return to the village and take her chances that someone there could get her to the castle. The second reminded her that she was a stranger here and only the Jadari knew she wasn't a threat.

Ashlee rubbed the space between her eyebrows. "I hope you know what you're doing." She wasn't sure if she meant the words for herself or the Jadari. Either way, she resumed her position against the wall.

The sucking began again and this time she didn't fight it. She felt herself being absorbed by the wall behind her. Panic filled her, but by the time she thought about once again moving away, the wall had already engulfed her too much and she couldn't break free.

Just go with it, she told herself. Taking a deep breath, she felt the edges of the wall close around her face.

CHAPTER 29

When Jayla regained consciousness, two things immediately entered her mind.

One: Coldness burrowed into every limb and two: she remembered her dream.

The dream itself consisted of every story she'd ever told, from the two brothers who'd each kept the same secret and had to face each other, to the jade beast surrounded by jeweled creatures under a green sun, to the beautiful Gemstone woman who'd peered at her through a crystal cage. In the dream, Jayla had been herself, standing on a stone platform, reciting each of her stories into the archway, which grew in size as if puffing itself up, like it needed to defend itself against her words.

Still, the words came through thick and strong, pouring out of her mouth. She spoke of her brother's demise at the hands of her father, the three friends who would cross two worlds to save one fairy, and the story of the lonely Gemstone woman who met the escaped princess and changed the world. Jayla didn't know why, but something in her stories held the key to collapsing the archway.

Now, awake, Jayla wondered why she'd wanted to destroy the archway so badly in her dream. True, she'd never liked the object in her father's quarters, but she'd never wanted it demolished. Yet in her dream she knew the importance, nay the *need* to keep speaking so it wouldn't continue to expand.

The remnants of the dream stayed with her for several moments until the coldness of her surroundings blotted everything else from her mind.

At that moment, she opened her eyes.

Her room, or cell as she determined it to be, remained dim in the weak light which shone through a few slits around the edges of the ceiling. *Must be almost morning,* she thought. Once her eyes adjusted, the walls sparkled a bit in the emerging daylight. She'd expected basalt walls or perhaps even the jade of her own castle, but this room appeared glittery and uneven. Scents of stale air and cleanliness reached her nose, as if the cell had not received many visitors, but had been cleaned recently for her arrival.

She must be in the Gemstone Dominion.

Jayla curled up in a corner, rubbing her arms and legs to push away the chill, and let hot resin tears fall down her cheeks. In the past week she'd lost her brother, run away from her home and father, turned into a grim-shu, and from the looks of things, somehow ended up in the Gemstone Dominion, cut off from everyone and everything she knew, and a prisoner on top of it all.

Hopelessness settled into her bones, amplifying the cold. She'd always been an optimistic person, but right now, she couldn't imagine how she could survive from here on.

Jayla lifted her head at the sound of the door opening. Light streamed through the sliver, then expanded, bathing the room. The person in the doorway stood silhouetted in the brightness. A warmth flooded through Jayla when whoever had opened the door held up a lava lamp.

"I was told you were awake," the voice said. Feminine, Jayla guessed from the tones. She wondered for a moment who would have notified this woman, since she'd only been awake for a few minutes. Perhaps a guard listening outside for movement?

"You were informed correctly," Jayla replied, forcing her voice to remain steady. Whatever her situation, she represented the Jade Kingdom and would not show weakness. She pushed herself up off the floor and stood. She found herself to be about the same height as her jailer.

"What is your name?"

"Where am I?" Jayla countered.

The woman didn't reply right away. "Gem Castle."

Jayla hid her gasp. She'd expected some basement in a lodging or outdoor storage facility from a local villager.

"How did I get here?"

The woman retorted, "What is your name?"

Jayla paused for a moment. It was a reasonable request. This woman had answered her question. Also, since she was devoid of her own clothing and only wore some sort of generic frock, she assumed the Royal seal on her arm had been noted. That must be why she'd been brought to the castle. No reason to keep up any pretenses. "Princess Jayla."

"You are the Jade King's offspring?"

"Yes. His daughter. Now how did I get here?" she said quickly.

A snort. "You are quite demanding, considering you are a prisoner."

"Am I?" Jayla retorted. "That's good to know. Does that mean I'm not allowed to ask questions?"

"It means...it means you will answer mine first."

"Fair enough. However, I am very cold and quite hungry. Would there be any way to remedy this before we begin an interrogation?" Her response would tell Jayla the disposition of the woman in front of her. Would she be kind? Cruel?

"Of course." The woman made a motion behind her body and two Jadari entered—one carrying a warming lava lamp and the other a bowl of food. They must have been waiting with these items right outside the room.

"Thank you," Jayla said, taking the bowl, then froze.

Jadari. Here. In Gem Castle.

She was so used to seeing them in the Jade Castle that she hadn't even registered she wasn't *in* the Jade Castle. How were Jadari *here*?

"What are you doing here?" she asked the nearest Jadari.

"Do not answer," the woman said.

Heat coursed through Jayla's face. "The Jadari belong to the Jade Castle. How did you come to have them? Are they your prisoners as well?"

"Of course not," the woman said in a rush.

Jayla wondered about the defensiveness in the woman's tone.

As if she'd realized she'd said too much, the woman quickly added, "But that's none of your concern. They won't help you, so don't try."

Jayla took a moment to finish scarfing down two spoonfuls of the mixture in the bowl. There was something tangy in the food, a substance she'd never tasted before, but she really enjoyed it. When the food slid down her throat, a heat moved through her, stronger than any lava lamp could warm her.

The sudden thought of poison crossed her mind.

But what would be the point of killing her before she was asked any questions?

Jayla shook her head. She'd never excelled in this area. Interrogation and resistance were always her brother's fortes.

The thought of him brought a lump to her throat.

"Listen," Jayla said, lowering the dish for a moment. "I have nothing else to lose. Ask me whatever you want. I will tell you the truth, to the best of my ability."

The woman cocked her head, still silhouetted in the doorway.

"You have no reason to believe me," Jayla continued, consuming another mouthful. "I understand that our peoples were sworn enemies three thousand years ago. But I also know that much has changed in the Jade Kingdom since the Diamond Mountains rose. I assume the same has happened here. As a Jade Royal, I can speak for my kingdom. I choose to be open."

Silence.

Jayla continued to eat.

Finally, the woman spoke. "I will confer with my associates

and return shortly."

Jayla raised her bowl in acknowledgement. "I understand. I'll be here when you are ready."

The Jadari left, leaving the lava lamp, and the woman closed the door behind her.

Immediately, Jayla resumed sitting and began to shiver, but no longer from the cold. She had no idea how the Gemstone people would respond to her presence. She couldn't even imagine what would happen if her father found a Gemstone person in their land.

But the question was, how did she get here? Somehow, she'd crossed the Diamond Mountains, but that couldn't be possible.

Jayla put the meal down and thought, forcing herself to remember. The last thing she could recall was standing in a shop with Basala and several Basalt people around her...

"No..." she whispered. But it had to be true. She'd become a grim-shu. She'd been told they lived inside the mountains. She'd been a grim-shu and passed *through* the Diamond Mountains!

The revelation rocked her.

How had she returned to her own body? Why was she herself again? She must have seen her reflection in the allotted amount of time after consuming the crystal-limestone paste.

A knock.

Jayla raised her eyebrows.

The door opened before she could answer, but she'd *definitely* heard a knock.

Why would she have knocked if I'm a prisoner? Could it be that this woman doesn't quite know what she's doing?

"I-we've decided to proceed under the banner of a truce. You are correct. It has been a long time since the war happened. A lot *has* changed on this side as well. Perhaps this should be viewed as an opportunity."

"It is hard to feel that way as your prisoner."

"Unfortunately, I cannot let you have free rein either. I offer a compromise. I, and two Jadari, will escort you to some quarters where you can clean and dress in alternate attire. During this time, we will talk. Do you agree?"

"Do I have a choice?"

"You can remain here."

Jayla gave a weak smile. "Lead the way." She stood and shook out her legs, then followed her captors from the cell.

Perhaps she will not be my captor for long. If I can earn her trust, or the trust of the other Royals, perhaps we can put to rest a long-standing hatred. But to what end? She couldn't return home to tell...to tell who? Her brother? He was dead. Her father? He wanted to keep her captive. Who could she talk to? Or perhaps she could create her own alliance, here, now, and bring about a new era with her own people.

A quiet snort emerged from her nose at these thoughts. She still had the problem of not being able to *get* home.

Regardless, she was here, now, in the Gemstone Dominion. The first Jade person from the opposite side of the Diamond Mountains in three thousand years. If she never returned home, she would have to make her life here, and having allies would be helpful.

One final thought crossed her mind: one week ago she'd never even been past the Jade Kingdom's borders. Since then, she'd been to the Marble Realm, the Basalt Territory, and now the Gemstone Dominion. Who knew what tomorrow would bring...

Though that thought should have felt important, the entire notion of where she was and her future fled from her mind when she stepped into the light and saw the woman in front of her. Her sapphire eyes poured into Jayla's and a different sort of heat rose throughout her body.

"You," Jayla whispered, raising a hand almost as if to touch the woman's face. She couldn't help herself. The pull of attraction to this woman, ever since she'd seen her in dreams, pushed all logic from her mind. "I've seen you be—"

Before she could finish her statement, a smaller pinkish woman entered the corridor.

"Where is my friend!" the pinkish woman demanded.

CHAPTER 30

Shon sunk down on his grandmother's couch in the 55-plus community condo, letting out a deep breath. He'd just spent the last hour in a meditative trance, thinking the same thing over and over again. *"Bekk. Remember the JadeSlagger. Picture it. Then, 'Emerge.' Use the throne."*

After five months of living in the Marvin Looshe Medical Facility, it felt strange to be once again in the real world. He'd taken in the surroundings of his grandmother's place, noting the family pictures on the walls. Shon recognized a few as cousins and aunts and uncles, from the photos his mom had in a box he'd found after she'd died. But Shon didn't fail to note that there weren't any of him and his brother.

His mother and grandmother had had a falling out about two years before Shon was born. His mother hadn't talked about it much, but Shon asked one day and she said their grandmother didn't approve of her marriage to a Greek Orthodox man. Shon thought that was so stupid at the time. His father didn't even really practice his religion. But apparently it didn't matter to his grandmother and communication had been reduced to birthday and Christmas cards or a meetup at a relative's wedding.

This strain went away the moment their parents died two years ago. Their grandmother had been sweet and helpful and doting, but that only lasted a few months. She didn't know how to deal with two teenage boys and promptly returned to her absence in their lives, unless necessary.

Because of this, Shon currently couldn't wait to find his own place and get out of here, with its stale cooped-up smelling air and its plastic-smelling furniture. But without a job first and some money, he'd be stuck here at least a couple of months.

Shon also had a feeling his grandmother didn't quite trust that after his release from the hospital he wouldn't have a meltdown or his head wouldn't start spinning around or something equally as crazy. So he'd mostly stayed quiet during the car ride, replying to any questions with basic pleasantries. He'd learned, for example, that tonight she played bridge at the community gaming room and it often ran late. Shon had grinned, hoping maybe he'd get some time to himself—something he hadn't had for months—but then cringed when she'd returned to the condo at 7:30 p.m. after her card game, told him he couldn't watch TV while she slept, and promptly went into her room and closed the door. Within about ten minutes he could hear a light snoring from her general direction.

Since that point in time, he'd focused on the message to his brother. Because he'd been able to hear Bekk, he hoped Bekk could hear him. He knew his brother and Vic would have to return to Yar Castle at some point to confront the Jade King. It was the only way to save Iyah. The Jade King would sap any resource he could, but not only that, he would continue to spread jade stone across Iyah, corrupting the world for his own needs, and changing it entirely.

But Shon knew Bekk wouldn't be able to stop the Jade King on his own, especially because of the Jade guards there. So the only way to beat the Jade King would be to use the throne's energy to create something which could defeat them all. The JadeSlagger, a creature Shon had learned about and created through his connection to the jade stone when he'd been in charge of the throne of Iyah, could do just that. So he'd sent the instructions to Bekk. He didn't know if it would work, but he wanted to give his brother any extra help he could.

While sitting on the couch, the latest attempt to send the message felt different. The words almost seemed to echo inside his own skull, as if hearing them through headphones. He sensed the message had reached Bekk, but he wished he could be sure.

Only one way to find out. He pulled out his phone and called Vic to see if he could meet up with him and Belle, to relay what he'd done.

Ring. Ring. Ring.

No answer.

Shon wasn't sure where Vic lived, or any of Bekk's friends for that matter, so he sunk into the stiff couch, defeated.

How do I find them? he wondered. A sensation of exhaustion flooded over him. Between all the rigmarole of paperwork, last-minute interviews at the hospital, dealing with his discharge, and the last hour of focused concentration, the weight of the day caught up to him.

I wish I could return to Iyah, he thought. The familiar gut-rumbling embers of anger stirred in his belly, but Shon took several deep breaths and kept the fury at bay. He knew where the feelings wanted to focus on—himself. He still struggled with guilt and shame over what had happened with his brother and his parents. He wondered if he'd ever forgive himself, but usually when he thought about that notion, he felt sick to his stomach. How could he ever get away from what he'd done?

The anger twisted inside him and changed once again into despair. Why had he thought he was healthy enough to leave Marvin Looshe? He wasn't ready to be on the outside.

Because you have to help Bekk if you can, his inner thoughts reminded him. *If you want redemption, if you want to sleep at all without thoughts of self-hatred, you have to do everything possible to make things better for your brother and his friends. So suck it up and do whatever needs to be done.*

Shon reached into his bag, shook out a pill from a bottle, and swallowed it dry. He needed to keep it together. Tomorrow, he'd try Vic again and if that didn't work, he'd go to the hospital where Ashlee and Belle were in comas. He believed someone in their families could direct him to Vic's house or Vic would show up at some point to visit.

Shon settled into the couch, the decorative pillow rough against his head and neck. But he didn't let it bother him. With a plan in his mind, he felt hope settle into his chest. He would fix the situation, somehow. He knew inside he'd give his own life to help his brother and his friends. He'd do anything to make things right...

Wisps of images floated through his mind as he fell into slumber—a cracked archway, slithering shadowy creatures reaching out for him, and the cold laughter of the Jade King.

CHAPTER 31

Bekk swallowed against the dryness in his mouth. He, Vic, and Ryf all approached the base of Yar Castle. Several greenish puddles surrounded the entrance. The castle wasn't quite covered with jade the way it had been when his brother had ruled the place, but Bekk could still see the tendrils and vines of the green stone seeping through the castle's natural rock. It wouldn't be long before the whole castle was consumed, but if Iyah was collapsing on itself anyway, would it matter? Perhaps the Jade King had solidified the castle somehow, protected it from the merging areas around him.

Only one way to find out.

"Ready?" he said to Vic. Bekk watched his friend nervously pat the afro on his head.

"Sure, man, sure."

"Okay. You focus on getting Belle. Ryf, your job is to wait until I call you, then distract the Jade King. At that point, I'll make for the throne."

Vic merely nodded.

I will be very fast, Ryf said.

Bekk smiled, but a hollowness in his belly betrayed his fear. He'd stood in front of these same doors one month earlier. At that time, he'd believed this place was only a dream, a figment he'd created to keep himself from growing up. He'd also had no idea what lay inside the castle. He could never have known he'd have to face off against his own brother.

And now, here he was again, but this time he knew exactly what he'd discover inside. The Jade King, the man who'd been manipulating Shon, the individual who wanted to save his own world by pillaging others and killing fairies to do so.

A lump caught in his throat, which had gotten too dry to swallow anymore. He gave a weak cough then said, "Okay. Vic, when we first walk in, hold onto my arm. The entrance is gonna look a bit strange." Pressure on his bicep indicated his friend had followed his command.

Ryf flew up to the door, placed a hand on it, and waited. Nothing happened.

"Dead?" Bekk asked.

She nodded.

"Who's dead?" Vic asked, a catch in his words.

"The door."

Vic's forehead furrowed.

"It's complicated," Bekk said, "but we don't have time to talk about it right now." He took a deep breath, pushed against the heavy door, and opened it enough for them to squeeze through.

"Here we go..." Bekk said.

The entranceway was just as Bekk remembered, with the

kaleidoscope sensation as doors upon doors seemed to overlap all at once. The pressure on his arm increased as Vic gripped tighter.

Bekk focused his thoughts on going to the throne room. The room in front of them appeared to constrict onto itself until only a stairway remained.

Vic's hold lessened. "What the hell was that?" he asked, peering around the room.

Bekk made his way towards the stairs, Vic close behind. Ryf hovered overhead.

"It's...I guess it's sort of like a safety measure," Bekk answered Vic. "The castle shows you every possible entrance option that the throne can create. You have to concentrate on where in the castle you want to go and it'll push out all the other doorways."

"I felt like I was stuck in some sort of optical illusion."

"In a way, I think you were." They reached the top of the steps and grew silent. More splashes of green liquid covered the space. Bekk could feel his heart pounding in his temples. They stood in front of the next set of doors, pale and dead like the ones at the entrance.

"Should we knock?" Vic whispered.

"I doubt he'd answer. But I don't want to go in and startle him."

"Maybe we could crack it and say who we are, that we just want to talk?"

Bekk nodded. He wiped his sweaty palms on his pants before pushing the door open a smidge. He stuck his face into the open area.

"My name is Bekk," he called out. "I'm here with my friend,

Vic. I live here in Iyah. We want to talk and make sure Belle is all right."

Silence.

"Maybe he's not in there?" Vic suggested.

A voice cut through the silence, deep and resonant.

"Proceed."

"Here goes nothing," Bekk muttered. "You stay here until I call you," he said to Ryf. She nodded a confirmation. "Let's go," he said to Vic. He shoved the door further open, straightened his shoulders, and entered.

The throne room looked exactly as Bekk remembered from a month ago, with jade slinking throughout its normally amber and golden floors and walls. Except this time the throne itself shone green with jade, having been transformed into the solid stone. A couple dozen melted guards dotted the ground between the entrance and the throne and a doorway hung as if suspended in midair. Not only that, but as Bekk stared across at the huge stone man sitting upon it, he got the strangest sensation that the throne was made for the larger being. It had always felt too big for himself, but the curve up the Jade King's spine and the width between its arms appeared perfect for the stone giant.

In fact, the entire grandness and hugeness of the room fit the current throne-holder much better.

Bekk's forehead furrowed. Had this place been made for a Jade person to rule?

Bekk shook away the notion. Whoever this castle had been built for, the throne had not been made out of stone. The jade currently corrupted it and that meant it didn't belong.

Heavy breathing could be heard next to him and Bekk gazed over at Vic from the corner of his eye. He could sense the tension from his friend, no doubt torn between demanding to know about Belle and the overwhelming feeling of seeing the vast room with such a large opponent at its other end.

Bekk refocused on the Jade King. "Hello," he said, his voice tinged with the edges of an echo.

"Who are you?"

Bekk's shoulders tightened. "Like I said, my name is Bekk. This is my friend, Vic. We've come to make sure Belle is all right."

"The girl." The words held no tone to them except recognition.

Bekk saw Vic's hands close into fists.

"Where is she?" Bekk asked.

"She has gone. I do not know where."

"Gone? What do you mean gone?" Vic said, his words accusatory.

"Easy," Bekk said under his breath. Bekk eyed the throne. He had to get the Jade King off it. He took a couple steps forward. "What we mean, is, did she leave the castle? Was she...okay...the last time you saw her?"

The Jade King sat still for a moment, his eyes boring into Bekk's. Bekk held his ground.

"Why should I answer you?"

"Why you—" Vic began, moving forward. Bekk restrained him.

The Jade King let out a laugh. "You would attempt to fight

me?"

"No," Bekk said as Vic shrugged off his grip. "We're just concerned about her, that's all. She's a friend of ours."

The Jade King leaned into the chair. "You have traveled for nothing. The girl is gone." He nodded at the doorway. "Vanished. Not of my doing. Someone tried to infiltrate this room using the archway in my world. They failed. When they disappeared, the girl disappeared as well, as did the arch. Only the doorway remains. As for her safety status..." he trailed off and gestured to a shadowy smudge behind him. "I couldn't say."

Vic shook. Bekk grit his teeth. "Thank you for the update."

"What now?" Vic whispered.

The Jade King spoke before Bekk could answer. "Since I have answered your question, perhaps you would care to answer mine?"

Bekk raised his eyebrows. "I'll try."

"I see you and your fairies gathered outside the castle. Are you planning an attack? If so, I can assure you, your efforts will be futile. My guards can more than handle a few flying bugs. Though I would be willing to work out a deal. In exchange for me letting you live, you leave me one fairy so I can access the doorways."

This was the time. He needed to stall. Bekk moved, closing in on the throne, but giving the impression he was merely looking at the doorway. "That sounds like a nice offer, but I'm not fooled. I know your guards are gone. We found their remains."

The look of surprise on the Jade King's face made Bekk inwardly fill with pride.

"Clever boy," the Jade King snarled. "Yet so foolish. You

forget, I still wield the power of the throne." The throne glowed beneath him, filling the space with green light.

Terror raced through him. "Run!" Bekk called out. He turned to follow Vic towards the exit.

"Entrap!" the Jade King yelled.

A beam of green light shot out of the underside of the throne and zeroed in on Vic. The young man stood stock still for a moment, frozen in time, and then appeared to be wrapped in some sort of translucent green glass. Bekk caught up to him and raced around to his front, staring through the cage at his friend's frozen face.

"Let him go!" Bekk demanded.

The Jade King laughed, the noise bouncing around the large chamber. "Why did you think you could come here and defeat me?"

Bekk hid behind the statue of his friend. "It's not like we had a choice with you pushing us in this direction."

Silence. "I do not understand."

Bekk struggled to get himself under control, hoping against hope that Vic was still alive or would wake up in the real world and disappear from his prison. Nothing indicated either would happen so Bekk continued to babble. "You know, causing the areas of Iyah to merge, so that we would have to come to the castle."

When the Jade King didn't respond, Bekk peeked out from behind his friend and stared at the king's face. The look of bewilderment was unmistakable.

"You don't know that's happening, do you?" Bekk asked.

"Of course I do, do not be absurd," the Jade King retorted, but Bekk had already seen the truth on the man's face.

"No, you don't. And if you're not causing it, then something else is." He glanced over at the doorway. "You said someone tried to break into the castle through the arch?"

The Jade King shifted in his seat. "Yes, but, she died. She didn't even make it into this world."

Bekk peered at the hanging door. "What's wrong with it? I've seen doorways before. They never had any cracks." In fact, the more he looked at it, the more he grew concerned. Not only was it cracked, but something appeared to be...oozing from the breaks. Though his legs protested, he forced himself out in the open and looked straight at the exit. "What is this place?" he asked of the image inside it.

The Jade King had scooted towards the edge of the throne, as if he'd moved forward to get a better look at the cracks himself. "My homeworld," he said, his focus on the frame.

"Are you trying to get home?"

"I was, yes. But after the woman attempted to break through, the doorway remained lodged where it is. I cannot get it to go away." While he spoke, he rubbed the throne's arms, as if drawing strength from them.

Bekk continued the conversation, keeping the Jade King's attention diverted, although he found himself wondering about this new development. If the throne's ability to call and remove doors had been tampered with, maybe that meant something had become broken within the energy processes of Iyah. That may explain the merging of areas.

"I think the problems are all an accumulation of you being

here," Bekk began slowly.

The Jade King snorted. "My being here was prophesized. I'm supposed to be here."

Bekk moved a bit closer. "But things are going wrong."

The Jade King focused on Bekk. "Perhaps it is of *your* doing."

Bekk's heart raced. He was about three steps away from the throne. "Okay then, here's the deal. I bring in a fairy and you go home. If Iyah restores itself, then we know it's because of you. If it doesn't, then you can return and I'll leave." The bluff felt ridiculous in his mouth, but he had no choice.

"You would sacrifice one of your own fairies to allow me passage home?" The Jade King let out a scoff. "Highly doubtful."

"No. I won't sacrifice anyone. I know how to access the doorways without having to kill the fairies."

The Jade King leaned closer. "How?"

"I won't tell you," Bekk said, shaking his head. "It's my leverage."

"How can I believe you then?"

"If I bring a fairy in here, I can open the doorway. That should be proof enough."

The Jade King remained quiet for several moments. "What guarantee do I have that you will not protect Iyah to keep me from returning?"

"You've gotten here before. Obviously, I can't keep you out."

Thump. Thump. Thump. The Jade King's fingers tapped against the chair. "I have a counteroffer. You must open the doorway so that I can acquire resources before I go home."

"I won't let you steal from somewhere else."

"Very well, what if I take the resources from my own world?"

Bekk frowned. "Why can't you just return home to do that?"

"I need resin to heal myself before I travel through the doorway. I had planned to send one of my guards to retrieve some resin, but it did not work. I need to collect some from my world and apply it to myself before I can go."

Bekk didn't trust this man as far as he could throw him, which would be negligeable, but the details were oddly specific to be completely untrue. Bekk glanced out the window and noted the purple haze approaching the castle. He didn't have any time to waste. And he had to get the Jade King off the throne.

With a hope that he wasn't making a colossal mistake, Bekk whispered, "Deal."

CHAPTER 32

Jayman leaned against the stone railing, hands shaking. He peered across the land that surrounded the Jade Castle and spread into the Cracked Fields. There, in the distance, marched about three hundred soldiers, gleaming white in rising sun, shining against the burnt umber grounds.

He could scarcely believe that less than two hours ago he'd shown up once again inside the castle after morphing through a jade wall, accompanied by Jadari. His guides had stood as a barrier between himself and the palace's guards until Jayman was able to finish speaking to them about the Marble forces on their way. Then the guards moved him to a room, with the permission of the Jadari, who seemed to show no loyalty to anyone except a Royal and, apparently, Jayman, and after about a half hour, the guard in charge, Jarura, visited him.

She explained that she'd sent out scouts who corroborated his claim.

"You risked much by returning here after escaping from our dungeon," Jarura had told him. "But your allegiance from the Jadari and the verification of your statement both prove you are an ally to the crown."

"Except the Royals aren't here..." Jayman had said slowly.

Shock flitted across her face. "How could you know that?"

"Everyone knows," he'd replied. "Why do you think the Marbles are coming? The Overlord will not miss the chance to seize an opportunity like this."

Jarura had paced around the room. Then, to his astonishment, she said, "You will help us coordinate our efforts to defend this castle."

Despite his protests and attempts to convince her of his absolute uselessness as a fighter or strategist, she escorted him to the castle's walls.

"We will set up our own defenses," she'd told him, "but we have an advantage they do not know about. We have you."

Once again about to contradict her, she held up her hand to silence him. "Along the Cracked Fields are sections of jade. We will need you to work with the Jadari, to mobilize them to attack the oncoming soldiers from behind. We cannot do this ourselves. The Marbles are much more well-equipped than we are. Not to mention the Jade King took with him three hundred of our guards and they have not returned either."

"What can the Jadari possibly do? They are no match for an army."

"There are pockets of gas that spurt up through the cracks. All the Jadari need to do is travel there, ignite the gas, and return. The fires will startle and scatter their soldiers. We can better defend against confused enemies."

So here he stood, waiting for the word from Jarura to begin the assault. All the resin in his body felt like it either pumped too hard or had drained from him. Both qualities unnerved him. He held onto the image of his Beloved in his mind to hold himself steady. If the Marbles took over the castle, no one would be safe.

"Jade Guard!" Jarura called out. "On my mark!"

Jayman glanced at the Jadari, who stared at him wide-eyed, but nodded at him in their confirming ways. One even placed a hand on his arm and Jayman felt a warmth move through him, an energy that made him feel lighter and stronger. Any doubt left him. Any tiredness melted away.

He felt ready.

Jarura screamed out, "FOR THE JADE KINGDOM!"

Jayman raised his fists in the air along with the other guards and let out an indecipherable yell as well. The Jade Castle gates opened and a slew of guards ran to meet the oncoming Marble soldiers. Jayman ignored the fray, worried that if he witnessed the carnage he would lose his new-found courage. Instead, he turned to the Jadari.

"You know what to do," he said. "I'll watch from here and relay orders."

The Jadari, about twenty of them, bobbled their heads in agreement. Over a dozen of them melted into the jade wall. After a few tense moments, Jayman could see fires bursting behind and amongst the Marbles. Cries of confusion could be heard throughout their ranks and sure enough, they split off in multiple directions.

The guards continued their fight, now on three fronts, splitting the soldiers even further apart.

Jayman gave orders to the Jadari about where they should pop up and the process was repeated over and over.

"The next mark, there, just to the north of—"

A heavy sack smacked Jayman in the face, knocking him off his feet. He fell backwards onto the ground with a thud. A thick layer of foul liquid bubbled out through the broken container and across his body. Within moments, Jayman could hear a hissing noise. Shortly after, his skin began to burn.

"Acid bombs!" a guard called out. She rushed over and sprayed some sort of foamy mixture across his body. It smelled of resin and something sweet he couldn't quite place. Regardless, he immediately felt cooler as the acid turned to ash on his body.

"Are you all right?" she asked, offering her hand.

He took it and stood, but before he could even respond, she was already off to spray another victim.

Fear returned. Jayman hadn't thought the Marbles would penetrate the castle walls, which they still hadn't, but he'd forgotten about their Acid Archers, known for their precise aim and deadly concoctions.

A Jadari near him tugged on his arm and he refocused. "Right. Okay. To the North..."

CHAPTER 33

The Gemstone woman in front of Jayla appeared as if for a moment she was going to let Jayla touch her face, but the interruption of the pinkish girl caused her to whirl away.

"I told you to stay where you were," the Gemstone woman snapped.

"And I told you my friend said she'd come back with you and she's not here. So where is she?"

Jayla, though thoroughly confused, couldn't help but be impressed by the courage of this smaller creature. She didn't know very many commoners who would speak to a Royal in such a way. But something seemed wrong. She didn't appear to be made of gemstone, at least not one that Jayla recognized. And her body parts moved strangely, as if she her skin weren't as solid as those made of stone. The closest guess Jayla arrived at was to assume the girl must be made of some sort of pale rose quartz, but quartz wasn't able to contain consciousness.

The Gemstone woman drew herself up to her full height. Even Jayla could feel the power emanating from her. "You will not address me in this way. Return to the quarters where I left you. I will speak to you when I am finished here."

The pinkish woman squared her own shoulders. "Listen, I don't know who you are and I don't care. All you stone people are the same. Your king is crazy and you are keepin' my friend from me. I want to know where she is. Now!"

Jayla's ears perked up. The young woman had used the term "king." In the Gemstone Dominion, the Royals were termed Emperor and Empress. The Marbles Realm used Overlords. The Basalt Territory had Sovereigns. But only the Jade Kingdom used the title of King and Queen.

"You know of a stone king?" Jayla cut in.

The young woman stared at her. "Yeah, I met him." She paused. "He looked a lot like you, actually. Green, I mean." She paused again. "No offense, I mean, if that's offensive."

The Gemstone woman remained stock still. "You have seen the Jade King?"

The young woman let out a sharp exhale. "Yes."

Jayla wanted to speak, to ask a million questions about her father, but shock controlled her.

The Gemstone woman's forehead furrowed, and she began to murmur. "How can this be? How can she have seen him?"

Jayla could feel the tension in the room spiking. "Please, everyone, let us take a breath. It would appear that we all want questions answered."

The young woman crossed her arms. "I'm not sayin' anythin' more until you tell me about Ashlee."

The Gemstone woman looked as if she might speak harshly again, but instead Jayla heard a slight grinding of her jaw. "Your friend is...at the village where I found Jayla."

The young woman eyed Jayla. "That's you? Jayla?"

"Yes," Jayla replied. "And you are?"

"I'm Belle." The young woman returned her gaze to the Gemstone woman. "Why is Ashlee still at some village?"

The Gemstone woman shifted her feet and twisted her hands in front of her. "She remained behind."

Belle's eyes narrowed. "On purpose?"

Shrewd, Jayla thought, impressed once again. This young woman would not be fooled.

"No. I left her there."

"Then let's go get her."

"Not until you answer my questions."

Belle moved her arms and placed her hands on her hips. "I'm not answerin' anythin' until I know Ashlee is safe and sound."

"It is too dangerous before the sun fully rises. We will retrieve her later in the morning." Jayla could hear a tinge of desperation in the Gemstone woman's voice. Jayla wondered at that moment why she wanted to wait. And the more she thought about it, the more she realized things were not quite right. No other Gemstone person had come to help, to keep watch over Jayla in the castle. No other Royal had presented themselves, nor helpers, nor...anyone.

"I'm not leavin' her by herself," Belle said, holding her position.

"She will be fine. The villagers will have taken her in."

"But you don't know that for sure."

Silence.

Belle's face grew even pinker. "You know, I was so excited when I first learned about Iyah and now these other worlds. I thought it was so great to see other creatures existed. But you're all just as stubborn and foolish as humans are."

Jayla's pulse raced. All thoughts of the strangeness of the lack of people in the castle fled from her mind. "Did you say Iyah?"

Belle eyed her again. "Yeah. That's where I was before I woke up here. With the Jade King."

The Gemstone woman leaned over, pleading in her eyes. "This is very important. Please. Do you know if he opened any other doorways to other worlds? Did he make any mention of a plan to infiltrate the Gemstone Dominion?"

Jayla's mind raced. So this was the Gemstone woman's concern, that her father planned to conquer her dominion. And yet, how did she know about his plans at all and about other worlds and doorways?

Before Belle could answer, a Jadari burst into the corridor, swaying and moving its hands.

The Gemstone woman stared at it, her eyes wide.

"What?" she asked. "That can't be. Show me." The Gemstone woman departed, leaving Jayla and Belle alone.

"What's goin' on?" Belle asked.

"I believe she is 'going' somewhere," Jayla replied, not quite sure what the young woman meant by her phrasing. "But as to where, I'm not sure." Jayla frowned. Should she take this opportunity to try and flee? After all, she was a prisoner here. And yet...

Jayla peered up and down the corridor, her focus once again on the lack of people. Granted, it could have been a low-traffic hallway, but still...it felt odd. This was her only opportunity to learn about what had happened here in the Gemstone Dominion over the past three thousand years. She couldn't let that opportunity slip by.

And, if she were honest with herself, she didn't want to leave without getting more information about the Gemstone woman.

"Well I'm not lettin' her out of my sight until she tells me where Ashlee is," Belle said, taking off after her.

Jayla peered after them, still torn. What was going on here?

A Jadari tugged at her arm. She looked down, surprised. They were usually not very tactile creatures, although, they were supposed to be mute as well and one had spoken to her just a week earlier to warn her about her father.

This one, it appeared, didn't want to speak, but it did motion for her to follow the other two.

"You are not loyal to me," Jayla said, "though how you came to be on this side of the Diamond Mountains, I do not know. So why should I listen to you?"

The small creature made several motions. Though some of them looked a bit different from the signals Jayla knew from the Jadari in the Jade Castle, she could understand the basics: Jayla was needed to help protect the kingdom and somehow her father was involved.

Jayla took in a deep breath. She had recognized the Gemstone woman from her dreams. From her visions. That must mean something. And if she hoped to repair her own kingdom there needed to be a relationship established between herself and the Gemstone people.

On the exhale, Jayla nodded to the Jadari. "Lead the way."

Several empty corridors later, Jayla arrived behind the Jadari at a room. They entered. Jayla found it difficult not to gasp at the number of volumes collected here. *They must document every single moment,* she thought, internally comparing the place with the Time Room in the Jade Castle where they catalogued major historical events.

But then her focus narrowed onto one item in the room: the archway looming in front of her.

"It's here, too," she muttered.

The Gemstone woman nodded. "It appeared at the same time as the growing of the Diamond Mountains."

"Just like ours..." Jayla studied the arch, still amazed at how it appeared to be part of the wall and as if it didn't quite belong at the same time. She squinted. "Except...the one in my father's chambers didn't look like this." She noticed cracks along its edging and a strange gray haze spilling around its borders. "It seems to be falling apart."

"It was not like this before," the Gemstone woman said, also inspecting the doorway. She suddenly spun and faced Jayla. "What have you done? How did you do this?"

"Do what? I've done nothing."

Belle chimed in. "I recognize this doorway. I saw it, or somethin' like it, with the Jade King. It didn't look broken like this.

Except..." she paused. "When that weird grey rock woman came in, it did appear to crack. Then there was this flash of light and I ended up here." She turned towards the Gemstone woman. "Jayla wasn't there. She had nothin' to do with it."

The archway...groaned. There was no other way to describe the noise.

"What is goin' on?" Belle asked, retreating a couple steps.

"I do not know," the Gemstone woman said, also moving a distance away.

Flashes of images appeared inside the archway. Strange lands Jayla didn't recognize. The archway in the Jade Castle always remained as black as the inside of a dead volcano. It never changed, never showed anything else.

"What...?" she managed.

Suddenly a wind gusted from inside the archway and whipped around the room. Belle's clothing blew around her while Jayla's own hair smacked herself in the face.

"We should leave," the Gemstone woman said.

The three of them turned to leave the room when the Jadari bolted away first, ran through the door, and slammed it shut from outside, locking them all in.

CHAPTER 34

Ashlee felt like her lungs were going to burst. She couldn't keep from breathing much longer.

I'm going to die inside a cave wall! Her mind panicked and fought against the natural instinct to breathe. *No you're not. HOLD YOUR BREATH!*

Fresh air suddenly hit her face and she gulped in painful gasps. Then, her eyesight returned, her limbs could move, and she fell to the floor. Pain shot through her knees and the palms of her hands as she smacked the ground. But she didn't care. She could feel. She could breathe. She could see.

ASHLEE!!

Yir's voice rang inside her head. Tiny hands grasped her arm and a small head buried itself in her chest. Ashlee had never been so glad to see the little green fairy.

"Oh my God, Yir!" She hugged the fairy, letting herself adjust to her new surroundings. "Am I in the castle?"

Yes. Belle woke up and read your letter. She then told me to stay here and went to find you. I haven't seen her for some time, but

I didn't want to leave. And I'm so glad I didn't because here you are! Yir pulled her face away, her eyes sparkling. Crystals clung to Ashlee's shirt, remnants of the fairy's tears.

"I'm so happy to see you. I don't know about you, but I'm ready to go home. Come on. Let's find Belle and get out of here." She remembered the look of disdain on the Gemstone woman's face as she left Ashlee at the village. "I don't think we're welcome here anymore."

Belle went this way. Yir flew from the room and Ashlee followed. They moved through a few corridors. While they searched, she used the time to work out a plan to leave, but she couldn't think of one. Perhaps the Jadari could help her or perhaps Gemna would be so glad to get rid of them she will actually help them go.

Finally, they came to a hallway where six Jadari stood outside a door, their bodies holding it closed.

Ashlee frowned. "What's going on?" she whispered to Yir.

I don't know.

Ashlee wasn't sure if she should approach them or not when a *bang* sounded against the inside of the room. She gulped. What sort of creature were they keeping locked in that room?

Then...

"Let me OUT of here!"

Ashlee's chest filled with warmth at the sound of that voice. "Belle!" she cried out. Disregarding any caution, she raced towards the Jadari. "Let my friend out," she demanded.

The Jadari swayed a bit. Ashlee had no idea what they were

doing. Other voices could be heard through the door, both feminine. One she recognized as Gemna's. They were calling out to leave and something about the archway?

"Please," Ashlee begged. "I have to help them. Why are you keeping them in there?"

Yir floated around Ashlee's head. *That's my home!* Suddenly, Yir's face grew pale as she fluttered in place.

"Are you all right?" Ashlee asked. "What about your home?"

I can hear them. The smaller green beings. In my head. They are speaking to me.

Ashlee didn't bother to wonder how, since she could hear Yir in her own head. Instead she asked what they were saying.

They say...it is a bit confusing. Their words are strange sometimes.

"Just try, Yir."

They say to save Iyah the prophecy must be fulfilled. Everything must be timed exactly right for the...for the sacrifice to work.

Ashlee started. "Sacrifice? What sacrifice?" She could still hear the calls from Belle and Gemna and the other woman inside the room. "Oh no. That archway isn't sacrificing *my* friend. Yir, tell them to move out of my way."

They say they cannot let them out. They are scared. They do not know how the archway can be penetrated. They do not have the power, but all the elements are in play. Ashlee, I don't understand!

Ashlee's mind whirled with thoughts. Her hands shook with fear at her next words. "Okay, if they won't let them out, can we go in? I won't leave Belle in there all alone."

A few moments passed. *They know you are important.* She paused. *Me too? Why am I important.* A couple more seconds. *They don't know. Just that three friends crossed two worlds to save one fairy.*

Ashlee vaguely remembered that phrase. "Shon told us that, in the hospital."

Yir shook her head. *They keep repeating the same thing. They sound frightened. They say time is almost up.*

Ashlee drew in a shaky breath. She had no idea what might happen next, but she didn't want to stand outside this door and listen to whatever it might be.

"Let us in," she said. A rash thought entered her mind. Reaching into her pocket, she retrieved the diamond prism. "If you want this to keep stopping the grim-shu, you'll let me in."

They say they won't need it anymore.

Yet, to Ashlee's amazement, the Jadari parted and opened the door a crack. With hands stronger than she would have imagined, they guided her and Yir through the doorway. The diamond slipped from Ashlee's grip as she fell right into Belle's outstretched arms. Yir flittered around their heads. The Jadari slammed the door behind them.

CHAPTER 35

Shon wasn't sure where he was. In all his dream-wandering and moving through other worlds, he'd never been to a place like this before. It should have been frightening. He couldn't really see. Except he didn't feel like he had to. He somehow could *sense* everything around him without needing a visual. His body tingled from the strangeness of the air, which felt like a cross between liquid and gas. The place was not uncomfortable, but it still didn't feel right.

Shadowy figures moved about him. Were they friend or foe? Shon couldn't sense any malicious intent, but he didn't quite trust them either.

The figures slithered around his body, brushing against his legs, arms, and face. They felt like silky feathers, light to the touch, and yet he even wondered if they were touching him at all.

He tried to speak, to ask where he was, but words failed him. Instead, a thought issued from his mind and sunk through his surroundings, like slow-motion ink seeping into sand.

"Where am I?"

Two shadowy figures came closer, hovering in front of him. He could feel their presence, calming and reassuring.

"We are the Guardians. You have a choice to make. You may stay, bound to this next world, or you may redeem yourself. One requires trust in letting go, the other trust in yourself. You must decide."

Fogginess clouded his mind. Two different shadows encircled him, soothing and...familiar. They reminded him of delicious home-cooked meals and being tucked into bed as a child.

He could stay here, with them. Be safe and...home. He would no longer struggle or fight. He could be happy again. Just by letting go.

But a single drop of liquid warmth bloomed inside him.

Redemption.

He would have to continue to fight. Continue to go on, after all the wrongs he'd done. Trust in himself again.

The conflict raged within him. To stay and be free or return to an unknown battle...

CHAPTER 36

Exhaustion overtook Jayman as he gave order after order. The Marble army had indeed scattered, but reinforcements arrived an hour into the battle. The Jadari were travel-weary, the Jade Guards spent. He didn't know how they could keep the oncoming forces at bay any longer.

As he rubbed his bleary eyes, he saw the strangest thing. *A storm?* No. The clouds moved. Huge shadowy shapes congregated and swooped around the Marble soldiers. Screams could be heard from their ranks as the wispy beings flew overhead, darting in and out.

"What are those things?" He heard someone call out.

"Smoke Hunters!"

A new type of fear circulated amongst the Jade Guards. Smoke Hunters had not been used in centuries, banished to the land near the Jade Volcano to the northeast of the Jade Castle. They were unpredictable and animalistic, enjoying the hunt more than caring about any consequences to their actions.

Who would have called them now?

"DO NOT FLEE," he heard a low voice boom. "They will only attack the Marbles!"

Jayman turned in disbelief. He recognized that voice. Sure enough, a Jade man with broad shoulders and skin cracked from age stood nearby.

"Taker Jayro!" Jayman cried out, raising a hand. Taker Jayro acknowledged him and waved him over. Jayman moved through the scurrying guards. Out of breath, he reached his recent companion.

"What are you doing here?" Jayman asked.

"I've brought aid." He pointed out to the grounds. Indeed, the Marble soldiers were dispersing, running away from the Jade Castle and the Smoke Hunters. Cheers could be heard throughout the ranks of Jade guards.

Jayman stared in disbelief, not wanting to take his gaze away from their victory. "But how?" he asked.

"I made a deal with the Smoke Hunters," Taker Jayro replied. "They are a part of this land, too, and would have been exterminated by the Marbles."

"Are they going to destroy them?"

"No. They were instructed not to harm them. Let the invaders scurry back to their realm and inform the Overlord that the Jade Kingdom will fight to protect itself, with or without Royals."

After several more minutes, when it became clear the battle had ended, Jayman strode with Taker Jayro into the castle while he explained how he'd arrived.

"Then the Jadari helped me melt through the walls and return here," he concluded. "I informed the Jade Guard about the Marble invasion and, after some convincing, we set up a defense. And you?"

Taker Jayro's eyes held the same weariness as Jayman knew existed in his own. "When the rumor of Princess Jayla's demise reached my ears, I immediately began to formulate a plan to assist. The Jadari came to me and I instructed them to bring me to the castle. Instead, I came out at the base of the Jade Volcano in front of the Smoke Hunters. I learned quickly to trust in the Jadari, that they'd brought me to the volcano for a specific purpose. After some quick thinking, I struck a deal with them to help us defeat the Marble soldiers."

"What was the deal?" Jayman asked.

"They are to be used as messengers for the Jade Kingdom, a quest or "hunt" for them and a relationship of trust with us. It is time to rebuild this kingdom."

Jayman shook his head in disbelief. He would have never been able to think like that on his feet. If anyone deserved to run the kingdom in the absence of the Royals, it was Taker Jayro.

As if the Jade guards also felt the same way, one of them approached.

"Taker Jayro," she said. "Come quick. Something is happening."

They trotted after her down the hallway. "More soldiers?" Taker Jayro asked while they moved.

"No. In the Jade King's quarters. The Jadari have become frantic, saying they need you, both of you, to help with the archway. I've never seen them so hysterical."

Soon they entered the Jade King's quarters. Jadari, scrambling around, immediately calmed at the sight of them. The archway stood there, still dark as the center of an ash storm, still putting Jayman on edge.

But something appeared different. Cracks had formed in the frame. A strange oozing smoke spewed from its edges.

"What's wrong with it?" Jayman asked.

The guard spoke up after watching the Jadari for a few moments. "They are motioning that, 'The time has come. Iyah will have its king.'" She frowned. "I don't have any idea what that means."

But Jayman remembered something. A story Jayla had told in his inn. A story of two brothers, both who wanted to help, but one became a villain instead. The other sacrificed his own life to banish his brother from the world. That world had been called...Iyah.

Then, the strangest thing happened. The blackness of the archway flickered. Images took the place of the usual darkness inside the framework, showing places he didn't recognize.

"Do you see this?" Taker Jayro said.

"Yes," Jayman answered, leaning a bit forward and narrowing his eyes. A few of the images looked a little familiar, like other areas of the Jade Kingdom or perhaps other villages. Then he saw Basalt vendors, Marble teachers, and even Gemstone workers.

Gemstone?!

"This is showing us other areas of our world," Taker Jayro said, excitement in his words. "We can use it to cross over the Diamond Mountains and retrieve resin. We are saved!"

"No," Jayman said, placing a hand on Taker Jayro's arm,

preventing him from moving forward. "You can't."

"Why not? I can see each place, clear as day."

A strangeness came over Jayman. One of the images showed a room with a Gemstone woman, two smaller pinkish women, and...

...Jayla.

Alive!

The image flashed away just as swiftly as it had appeared. "The worlds are changing too quickly," Jayman said. "If you try to move through, you may be torn apart." He looked again at the archway. Each time the scene switched, the frame creaked and stretched, creating more cracks. "I think the archway is breaking apart. I think it's linking to other worlds, but the strain is too much. It won't be able to sustain the changes."

"Then what do we do?" Taker Jayro asked.

CHAPTER 37

Bekk wiped his sweaty hands on his pants. He called for Ryf and she fluttered into the throne room. He continued watching the Jade King, noting the greed in his eyes.

"Ryf, I need you to open the doorway, but I don't want him to see how," Bekk said.

Okay. I will turn around and get crystals and then open the door.

Ryf turned away.

"What is she doing?" the Jade King demanded, standing up.

Bekk held his breath. "I told you, she has a way to open the doors without the loss of her life."

The Jade King remained silent, but did not resume sitting.

Bekk licked his lips. As soon as the Jade King moved to enter the doorway, he'd grab the throne and create the JadeSlagger as a distraction. He thought for a moment about pushing the Jade King through the doorway and being done with him, but he worried he wouldn't be strong enough to push a huge man made of solid stone.

Ryf faced them again, her fist closed around what Bekk knew

contained a crystal.

Ready, she said to Bekk.

"She's ready," he repeated to the Jade King.

"Open it," he said, a dangerous edge to his voice.

Bekk nodded to Ryf.

Ryf moved towards the doorway and applied the crystal. The door glowed and hummed for a moment, then the image inside appeared even more real than before.

"It's open," Bekk told him. He peered through the doorway, noting a reddish amber liquid flowing over the rocks, near the edge of the threshold. The Jade King would only have to grab one and bring it through. He wouldn't have to go all the way in.

The Jade King must have realized this too, because when he approached the doorway, he knelt. Placing a hand against the edge, his arm slipped through the entranceway. With a smile, he retrieved a rock.

"Brilliant," he muttered.

At that moment, two things happened at once.

The first, was that Bekk reached out and grabbed the throne. He meant to call for a JadeSlagger, but as soon as his hand touched the chair, a sense of cold death rushed through him. He could not control the power of this throne. It had been tainted by the Jade King.

The second was that as soon as he touched it, a creature entered the throne room. Bekk recognized it from when his brother had been in charge of the castle. Sort of like a glass-blown scorpion with a spiked tail of jade. It had come after him and Yir had protected him, getting captured instead. Now, in its grip, it carried a plump purple fairy.

King Fai.

Father! Ryf cried out.

"Ryf don't!" Bekk called to her. But it was too late. He couldn't move towards her because his hand had gotten stuck to the throne. Tiny pinpricks stabbed at his fingertips, as if the throne were sucking the life out of him.

Time seemed to slow. Bekk could see everything with such clarity: from the look of triumph on the Jade King's face to the details of Vic's shoes encased in the jade stone to the look of fear in Ryf's eyes as she fled to help her father.

"I told you, you were a fool," the Jade King snarled at Bekk. "You place your trust in others, just as I did. They will always let you down, run away, betray you. I trust only in myself now. I discovered my own methods for obtaining fairies. I have no need for you or your treachery," he said, pointing at Bekk's hand on the chair.

Bekk couldn't respond. He had no words left, no energy. The throne glowed a sickly shade of green, draining him, drowning him in darkness.

I'm going to die for real this time, he thought. A random flicker of hope popped into his mind. *At least I'll see Mom and Dad again.*

Suddenly, a sound began, as if the wind had teeth and crunched on the air around it. The throne vibrated beneath him and a burst of green energy shot from it, moving through him, and shining onto the doorway across from him. The noise continued, like the grinding of stone, and a spot of blackness appeared inside the entrance. It grew, seeming to consume the space around it, expanding and suffocating its surroundings until it fully transformed into the archway.

That's where I'm going, Bekk thought in his delirium. *I'm going to die.*

Except the blackness didn't stay. Other images flashed through the arch. Images of other worlds Bekk didn't recognize. Some appeared green like jade, others dark gray or shining white. A third appeared like jewels that would make anyone drool at their worth. Then the darkness again, but with shadowy figures moving about inside it.

"What are you doing?" the Jade King demanded, approaching Bekk. "Stop. Now! I order you!"

Bekk couldn't tell him it wasn't him. No voice existed within him anymore. He fought just to remain conscious.

"I said STOP!" The Jade King reached Bekk, grabbed him by the arm, and yanked him away. He was surprised he hadn't lost his hand to the throne. Instead, he felt himself flying away from the chair and sliding towards the archway.

When the inky blackness became visible again inside the archway, a dual voice whispered to him from inside. A sense of comfort enfolded him. A feeling of home.

"We will protect you. Embrace the archway. Trust us."

CHAPTER 38

Wind swirled around Jayla and she could barely see. Suddenly something sucked at the room, pulling all its contents towards the archway.

"Hold onto something heavy!" she screamed. She reached out and grabbed hold of the desk next to her, clawing to get a grip on the slick gemstone surface. Finally she dug her fingers into some of the grooves and held on for dear life. Her eyes widened with terror as even the desk slowly slid its way towards the blackness of the arch.

Out of the corner of her eye she saw someone enter the room and barrel into Belle. The new addition looked similar to Belle, except with lighter hair and some sort of small sparkling green creature attached to her. They fell onto the floor, sliding towards the archway.

"Help them!" Jayla cried out, but the Gemstone woman could barely hold onto the shelving unit next to her. Jayla could see her fingertips stretched to their capacity, a look of horror on her face.

The two young women with the green creature smashed into the Gemstone woman, whose grip failed. She went flying towards the archway, screaming.

Without thinking, Jayla let go. She flung herself onto the floor, crawling next to the two young woman, who'd lain flat and were out of the major drag of the wind.

The Gemstone's woman's eyes were wide with fear.

Jayla reached out to hand. "Take my hand. Trust me."

*

Ashlee's screams were lost in the wrenching wind coming from the arch. She clung to Belle and Yir, laying face up on the ground.

There. She saw something inside the archway. A flash of an image. She saw Bekk struggling with a huge Jade man.

Everything made sense. She had all she needed. Or at least, she hoped...

She peered over at Belle. "Trust me!" she yelled. She took Belle's hand and sat up. With her other hand, she grabbed the crystals Yir had cried on the front of her shirt. The archway swept all three of them forward.

*

The Jade guard and Jadari had vacated the Jade King's quarters, leaving only Jayman with Taker Jayro.

The images inside the archway kept moving, but seemed to be slowing a bit in their cycle. Then, only the same two images began to alternate: one of the Jade King fighting with a young man made of some sort of yellowish stone while the other showed Jayla and the Gemstone woman.

A thought struck him and a plan formed in Jayman's mind.

"Just do what I do when I say. Trust me," he said to Taker Jaryo.

*

Jayla grabbed the Gemstone woman's hand and with all her might, she pulled her from the void. The momentum swung Jayla around and she tripped over Belle on the floor. Floundering backwards, her body hit the archway, with the two girls at her feet. Something grabbed her from inside the archway and yanked her into the void. A bright light surrounded her, brighter than any lava spew.

The last thing she saw in that room was the Gemstone woman's eyes wide, not with fear for herself, but with both gratitude at being saved and helplessness as Jayla was sucked inside.

*

Ashlee screamed the whole way as she slid into the darkness of the archway, gripping the crystals in her hand and Belle's arm with the other. At the very moment she hit the archway, light shone from inside, brighter than the diamond used to fend off the grim-shu.

*

The Jade King charged Bekk.

"I will be ruler of this land!" he shouted.

Bekk knew he was going to be pushed through the archway. He had no energy left to fight. Instead, he closed his eyes, and believed in the voices that told him to trust...

As soon as he felt the Jade King come in contact with him, he grabbed on. He felt himself being pushed into the archway. More snaps and cracks sounded around him. He could see over the shoulder of the Jade King, view the purple haze of the infiltrating Iyah region reach the edges of the castle's windows.

Then bright light, brighter than the sun, surrounded him. He closed his eyes and let out a soundless yell.

*

The Jade King let out a howl of rage and charged the boy, struggling with him against the archway. He had it, he had everything. He didn't need anyone else.

The world at his fingertips.

The universe as his playground.

He could be both a monster and a savior.

Then bright light blinded him.

*

Shon knew what he had to do.

Swirling inside the foggy blackness, he felt a sense of complete clarity. Every world spun before him, yet he could see them distinctly. Each point, coming together in perfection.

I trust me.

As soon as the thought was released into the void, the space around him began to brighten, growing lighter and lighter until he had to shut his eyes from the intensity of the illumination.

CHAPTER 39

Jayla opened her eyes with a start. She let out a moan. Waves of pain pulsated through her, but thankfully lessened with each moment.

"Jayla?" a voice called out.

The aches diminished even further and normality returned.

"Yes," she managed, coughing the word out. Her vision adjusted to her surroundings. Instead of gleaming gemstones she saw intricate shades of jade green in the walls. Two men stood above her, their skin similar to her own. She was home.

She recognized the one to the left right away. "Innkeeper Jayman?"

He nodded, helping her to sit up.

Suddenly, a rumble could be felt through the floor. They'd had earthshakes like this before, with all the volcanic activity on their world, but nothing like this. Her teeth chattered inside her skull. She watched Jayman and the other man lose their own balance and land unceremoniously on the floor near her. The tremor continued for several minutes, then abruptly ceased.

"What was that?" she asked, her head spinning.

"I'm not sure, Princess," the other man said, his voice low and gruff. It seemed familiar to her.

As her vision cleared, she peered into his face and recognized him from that night at the inn. "Taker...Jayro, correct?"

"Yes, Princess."

The three of them got to their feet. "What are you two doing here?" she asked both men.

They recapped their exploits: Jayman's arrest, Taker Jayro's rescue of him with the Jadari, Jayman's time with the Basalt woman and then alerting the Jade Guard about the Marbles' invasion, and Taker Jayro's deal with the Smoke Hunters.

As Jayla absorbed how much had happened since she'd fled the castle a week ago, she noticed something amiss in her father's quarters.

The archway was gone.

She'd never seen the room without it. With delicate movements, she traced the wall where it had been. Somehow, she'd been transported through it when she'd switched places with the Gemstone woman, which allowed Jayman and Taker Jayro to bring her through into the Jade Kingdom.

Jayla's thoughts went to the Gemstone woman. She'd never seen anyone so beautiful. And she'd been so close to establishing peaceful ties with her. Now Jayla found herself stuck once again, an impenetrable barrier between herself and the woman.

She'd never even learned her name...

"One other thing, Princess," Taker Jayro said, removing an

object from a sack on his shoulders. It glittered underneath the overhanging chandeliers.

The Gemstone Book.

"I believe I am supposed to present you with this," Taker Jayro continued, bowing slightly as he handed it over.

Jayla took it gingerly, caressing the colorful cover. An idea sprung to mind...

Suddenly, a Jade guard came running into the room.

"Princess Jayla!" she squeaked, obviously not expecting Jayla's recent arrival.

"Do you have news?" Jayla said, immediately resuming her role as a Royal.

"Yes, Princess. The rumors have floated quickly. The Diamond Mountains have crumbled and fallen within the past hour! The barrier between lands has vanished!"

Jayla understood the severity of those words. If she didn't act quickly, things could go awry in days, perhaps hours.

"Send out this decree to all the land," she said, her mouth a bit dry. She began to speak a lie she hoped would become truth. "I have come into a peaceable agreement with a Royal of the Gemstone Dominion. This book is proof of that. We are no longer enemies. Each Jade citizen is to remain in their own land areas until myself and the Gemstone Royal meet in...three days time. Is that understood?"

The Jade guard nodded and strode from the room.

Jayla placed a hand to her forehead, suddenly weak. She took a seat on her father's bed.

My father...

She wondered where he was, if he would return.

With a slight shake of her head, she put the thought behind her. Regardless, she was in charge. And there was work to do.

With a clarity she hadn't felt in a long time, she stood and addressed Taker Jayro first. "You are now in the service of the Jade Royal family," she began. "I task you to help orchestrate a peaceful transition between ourselves and the Gemstone Dominion. You will accompany me in three days to set out for their land."

Taker Jayro paused. "Did you really speak with a Gemstone Royal?"

"I did."

He let out a long breath. "I wanted to believe, but truthfully, I did not think it would happen. And yet here you are, alive, and leading our kingdom into peace." Tears formed in his eyes. "I will return in two days, Prin...Queen Jayla, after I've completed all preparations for my departure at the institute." With those words, he exited.

"Queen..." she muttered. That word spoke the reality of the situation. With her father and brother gone, she now commanded the Jade Kingdom.

"Jayla...er, Queen?" Jayman said.

Jayla smiled. "I prefer if you'd call me Jayla," she told him.

He grinned. "Thank you, Jayla. I would like to ask to return home. I haven't seen my Beloved in days."

Jayla's smile lessened. "I cannot allow that. I need you here."

"But—"

She cut him off. "You have proven yourself more than an innkeeper. Even when we knew you, you were generous and caring. And what you did for the kingdom, risking a return to the castle, even after being arrested, to warn the Jade Guard...I need someone like you to help me in the coming months, perhaps years, as we transition into peace. However," she finished, the smile full bloom once more, "you *and* your Beloved are welcome to live within the palace during that time."

Jayman's eyes lit up. "Me? Live here? In the palace?"

"You always said you'd dreamed of this place."

Jayman straightened. "I would be honored to help you, Jayla." With a short nod of his head, he moved to leave.

"One last thing," she called out. "I believe there is a certain Basalt woman who lives in Bajay we have both met. I'd like you to extend an invitation to her to join us at the castle to thank her properly for her assistance. And, if for no other reason, than to learn her name."

Jayman smiled broadly, then let out a whooping laugh before exiting the room.

Jayla let out a deep exhale. She may have a long road ahead of her, but she wasn't alone.

CHAPTER 40

Bekk opened his eyes with a start. He took a few moments to get his bearings. A tingling flowed through him where he sat, which was on the floor of Yar Castle.

Except, the throne room had changed. Instead of the normal amber he'd come to know or the jade which had seeped throughout the grounds, the floor appeared multi-tonal, made of a million types of stone, rock, gem, wood, metal...he couldn't even name them all. The throne, also, appeared the same way, glowing and pulsating in a multitude of colors. The room felt warm and inviting, not large and echoey like before.

The place felt...whole.

Bekk pushed himself to his feet and turned. The archway had gone. Vic's body, frozen in jade, had vanished. The odd scorpion-like creature which captured King Fai had disappeared. Only three other beings existed in the room: King Fai, shaking his head as he sat up, Ryf, hovering over her father, and a large-bodied man lying on the floor a few steps away.

Bekk recognized his shape and knew it must be the Jade King, but his body appeared the same as the floor and throne, no longer merely jade, but a composite of every type of material possible.

Not quite sure if he should check on the new version of the Jade King or flee while he had the chance, Bekk's decision was made for him as the man began to rise.

Bekk retreated several paces, inserting himself between the huge man and the two small fairies behind him.

The composite man turned, stretched out his limbs, admiring them.

"This is not what I expected," the composite man said. His voice sounded the same as the Jade King's, and yet...Bekk recognized something else in that voice.

Not something...someone.

His brother.

"Shon?" Bekk whispered.

The composite man turned his head and saw Bekk. "Yeah, Bekk, it's me."

Bekk paused for a beat, then raced across the room and embraced his brother. He'd expected hardness and resistance from the body, but he felt normal, like his brother would feel.

"I'm so sorry," Shon said, engulfing him in a hug, "for everything."

"But how?" Bekk said, pulling away.

"I'm not quite sure. I was inside the archway and I knew that if I chose to, I could stay there. I felt at home, at peace. But I heard a voice, or two voices at the same time, also giving me another option. A way to redeem myself." Crystals welled up in Shon's new eyes. It appeared the gift of the fairies to open doorways had been bestowed upon his brother now.

"But what does that mean?"

Shon bowed his head to Ryf and King Fai. "If they will allow it, I'd like to help restore Iyah."

King Fai inclined his own head in return. *In your blood lies the true King of Iyah,* King Fai said. *I believed you were to lead us, Bekk, but now I see differently. Your brother was always meant to be here. He had simply gone astray. But his true self has been revealed and accepted by the castle. It has been restored.*

I always liked him, Ryf added.

Bekk laughed. Then he noticed Shon laughed, too. "Wait, you could hear them now?"

Shon quieted. "I guess so." He nodded in the direction of the fairies. "I will not fail again. I promise."

"And the collapsing of Iyah?"

"Fully restored," Shon replied.

Bekk stared at his brother's new body. "Why do you look like this? And what happened to the Jade King?"

Shon slowly rubbed his hands over themselves, as if taking them in. "It was strange. A bright light blinded me, but I could still see through it. In front of me, every single world opened at once. I felt whole, and finally at peace. I made my choice to return. The kaleidoscope of worlds consumed me, but at the same moment, a figure crashed into me. It was the Jade King."

Shon peered over at where the archway had been. "He felt like pure rage. I recognized the feeling right away—I've fought it my whole life. Anger at life, at failure, at loss. We grabbed onto each other and...his color melted away into the darkness. His body filled with...well...whatever I am now, and my being or essence or whatever you want to call it flooded into the empty shell of his body. Then I felt pain and heat and suddenly I was on the floor, here." He returned his gaze to Bekk. "And I saw you. Alive and okay, but still here in Iyah."

Shon then got down on his knees, so he could look Bekk in the eye. "Bekk, I don't deserve forgiveness, after everything I did, but I am really sorry. I was an idiot. I felt so guilty about Mom and Dad and thought if I could help them be alive again, I could make up for things.

"But I was wrong," he continued. "I should have been happy that I knew they were okay, wherever they were, and focused on letting go and forgiving myself." He placed a hand on Bekk's shoulder. "I'm mostly mad for what I put you through. You should never have had to stop me in Iyah, especially not the way you did. I can't forgive myself for that, but maybe I can do right somehow in this world for other children who need this place."

So many emotions whirled through Bekk he didn't know where to start. Anger, of course, at everything that his brother had done and yet gratitude for helping his friends. Shame and disappointment and pride all roiled around inside him. "Well, at least there's one thing that won't be too bad. I won't be here alone anymore."

Shon smiled and Bekk could see his brother in the composite man's eyes. They were full of love and life.

"That's not *quite* true..." Shon said. He raised his hand and brought it over Bekk's face, creating a strange glow that turned into darkness.

"Shon...what are you—"

Heat poured through him. Images floated past his eyes of events that had just taken place. And then the blackness overtook him.

CHAPTER 41

I see Ryf...!

Ashlee's eyes opened with a start, Yir's words echoing through her mind. The last thing she remembered was praying she'd made the right decision by going into the archway with the fairy crystals in her hand. Her current surroundings and the message from Yir made her realize she had. With the use of the crystals, she'd been able to penetrate the archway because it was broken, and Yir returned to Iyah while she...

...white walls, a beeping monitor, and the faces of Vic and Belle confirmed it...

...she was home.

Tears sprung from her eyes.

"Hey," she said with a wheeze.

"OH MY GOD!" Belle leaped out of the hospital chair and flopped herself onto Ashlee's bed, squeezing her tight. Vic also moved over, patting her shoulder, a huge grin on his face.

"I knew it," Belle said, her voice muffled by her face being engulfed in the blankets. She pulled away. "I knew that when I woke up you would wake up, too. Vic was already in my room, visiting, so as soon as we cleared it with the doctor, she let me come over."

Ashlee noted that Belle also wore a hospital gown. All of her own muscles felt sore and heavy. "Why am I, are *we,* here?"

Vic answered. "After the second visit to Iyah, you didn't show up with us and when we woke up, you didn't. You were in a coma. It's been four days."

"What? But I was only in that gemstone world for a day and a night."

"Time works differently in other worlds, remember?" Belle said, smoothing down Ashlee's hair.

"So what happened? Why am I here? What happened with the gemstone world and with Iyah and Bekk?"

"We don't know, hon," Belle said. "When you pulled me towards the archway, the last thing I remembered was a really bright light and then I woke up here in the hospital."

"What happened with the Jade King in the castle?" Ashlee asked Vic. "Did Bekk beat him? Did he win?"

Vic shrugged, his tone sad. "I don't know."

"Well we have to go back," she said, her voice rising. "We can't leave him there alone."

At that moment, her parents walked through the door. Their greetings and gestures of love halted any conversation between herself and her friends.

But a strange sense kept enveloping Ashlee, from the time she woke up, a feeling that she wouldn't be able to return to Iyah. She'd somehow known it already, the night she ended up in the gemstone land instead. She wasn't meant to return to Iyah ever again.

Later that day, after a few more tests that showed nothing wrong, her parents drove her home, gushing over her miraculous recovery, and promising to be around more often. Ashlee barely heard them as detachment swept over her. She'd worked so hard to help Bekk, to help the Gemstone woman, to help Yir. But had it done any good?

That night, she fell asleep thinking of Iyah, but when she woke the next morning after a dreamless night, she knew her efforts to return there were over. Whatever she'd been meant to do had been concluded. Iyah didn't need her anymore.

Waves of grief crashed into her at the thought of Bekk. The day of his funeral, when she'd seen Yir, she'd let something inside her burn with the tiniest mote of hope that he was somehow alive. And then she'd seen him on the beach in Iyah, touched him, kissed him. For a few brief moments he *had* been alive again.

But now he was gone. Forever.

Ashlee allowed the tears to come freely.

Her parents insisted she stay home from school the next day, seeing as how she'd just returned from the hospital. They took off work, too, and watched movies with her, had the cook make her favorite meals, and told her she could do anything she wanted to that day.

"I just want to rest," she told them. She trudged to her room, shut the door, and lay on the bed, hugging a pillow and letting tears run down her face.

Several minutes later she heard a tentative knock at her door.

"Honey?" her mom called out. "You have a friend who stopped by to see how you are. Are you up for a visitor?"

Ashlee sniffled and wiped her tear-stained cheeks. Perhaps Belle's mother had also let her stay home from school and she'd come to visit. Ashlee didn't really want to talk about anything, but she knew Belle was one of the only people on this planet who would understand how she felt.

"It's okay, Mom, let her in."

The door opened and her mom stood in the way. "Recovering or no, this door still stays open."

Ashlee sat up, confused by the statement.

Her mom moved out of the way and Ashlee understood the mentioning of the rule. A young man stood in the doorway, a bit older than herself, with a slightly gaunt face and dark hair.

Bekk's brother, Shon.

"Hey Shon," she said, clearing her throat. "What are you doing here?" She paused. "Wait, what are you doing *here*? Why aren't you at Marvin Looshe?"

"Released," he replied, his voice a bit rough.

Ashlee peered over at her mom. "It's okay, Mom. It's Bekk's brother."

"Oh, all right. Not too long of a visit, though. You need your rest." Her mom walked away down the hall.

"Thanks for checking to see how I am," Ashlee said, motioning for him to sit at her desk chair.

He didn't move. He just stared at her.

"What?" she asked.

He entered slowly into the room, reaching out to touch her face.

She retreated a little and he paused.

"Shon? What's going on?"

He stared at her, long and hard.

Her breath caught in her throat. His eyes. Something about his eyes... She recognized someone else...

"Bekk?" The word came out in barely a whisper.

He gave a tiny nod, as if he couldn't believe it himself.

Ashlee patted on the bed this time for him to take a seat next to her. He did, his body only a foot away from her.

"It...it can't be you," she said. Her heart pounded in her chest.

"It is."

She raised her own hand and very gently traced his jawline. It was definitely Shon's face, but there had always been similarities between the brothers. His eyes though...they were definitely Bekk's eyes...

"How?"

"My brother sent me to Earth, into his body. He stayed in Iyah. He's taken over the Jade King's body, but he's different now. He's going to rule Iyah." Bekk paused. "I think he was always *meant* to rule Iyah."

Ashlee remembered the words. "There was a prophecy. Shon said he heard it. That 'three friends would walk upon two lands to help one fairy and save all worlds. That they knew the king of Iyah and his reign would come about through the void.' I didn't know what it meant. And then when the Jade King took over, I thought it meant *you* would become the king. But it was your brother all this time. We all knew him. And when I crossed to save Yir and brought her through the archway, it broke the arch, didn't it?"

Bekk nodded. "Before my brother sent me here, he showed me all that had happened. You had to follow Yir to help the Gemstone woman so she could meet the Jade woman and bring about peace. Belle had to find you in the Gemstone Dominion so that when the archway began to collapse, you knew it was your only chance to cross back through."

"I remembered about the fairy tear crystals, that they open doorways. At least, I hoped they would."

Bekk went on. "Well, you did it. Yir's crystals combined with the cracked archway broke open all worlds. You were sent to Earth with Vic and Belle, I was in Iyah with Ryf and Shon, the Jade woman returned to her kingdom and the Gemstone lady remained in her dominion."

Ashlee shook with disbelief. "All those moments had to happen on their own so that they could come together. It's insane."

"A lot of different individuals, from stone people to fairies, did their part to make sure the prophecy would be fulfilled." He reached up and slowly tucked a piece of loose hair behind her ear. "But you each had to decide to be a part of it. If any of you had changed your minds, this wouldn't have worked."

"We did it for you," she beamed.

"Then I better make it worth your while..." Bekk leaned in to kiss her.

She stopped him, her eye on her open door. "This will be a scandal, you know, me with Bekk's older brother. I mean, you are three years older than me now."

He smiled and trailed a finger across her lips. "Then I'll wait for you and we'll take things slow. I promise...I'm not going anywhere..."

FROM THE AUTHOR

Thank you so much for reading the
Land of Iyah trilogy!

I cannot express how grateful I am that you've traveled with me through the *Land of Iyah* trilogy adventure. I hope you enjoyed reading these books as much as I enjoyed writing them. I had an absolute blast!

If you've enjoyed these books, please consider sharing them with others.

Thank you again!

~Christa Yelich-Koth

ABOUT THE AUTHOR

Christa Yelich-Koth is an award-winning author (2016 Novel of Excellence for Science Fiction for ILLUSION from Author's Circle Awards) of the Amazon Bestselling novels, ILLUSION and IDENTITY. Her third book in the *Eomix Galaxy Novel* collection is COILED VENGEANCE.

Christa has also moved into the world of detective fiction with her international bestselling novel, SPIDER'S TRUTH, the first in the *Detective Trann series*. Looking for something Young Adult? Try the YA fantasy *Land of Iyah* trilogy, starting with book 1: THE JADE CASTLE.

Aside from her novels, Christa has also authored a graphic novel, HOLLOW, and 6-issue follow-up comic book series HOLLOW'S PRISM from Green-Eyed Unicorn Comics. (with illustrator Conrad Teves.)

Originally from Milwaukee, WI, Christa was exposed to many different things through her education, including an elementary Spanish immersion program, a vocal/opera program in high school, and her eventual B.S. in Biology. Her love of entomology and marine biology helped while writing her science fiction/ fantasy aliens/creatures.

As for why she writes, Christa had this to say: "I write because I have a story that needs to come out. I write because I can't NOT write. I write because I love creating something that pulls me out of my own world and lets me for a little while get lost inside someone or someplace else. And I write because I HAVE to know how the story ends."

You can find more about Christa and her other books at:
www.ChristaYelichKoth.com